ANOTHER SLICE OF FEAR

...Short Stories of Suspense and Terror

BY ANDREW ALLEN SMITH

Another Slice of Fear

Short Stories of Suspense and Terror

By Andrew Allen Smith

For more information, please go to AndrewAllenSmith.com

All names, characters, businesses, events, incidents, strange shopping stores, mysterious bookstores, and other stuff in this story are fictional. Any similarity with a person, place, or thing, living, dead, undead, free-floating spirit, vengeful wraith, or other malevolent or protective entity is purely coincidental and the product of an overly healthy, yet sometimes a little over the top, imagination.

Dedication

To Kylie and Dana, who have faced the depths of real fear and continue to overcome it each day.

Authors Rant

So here we sit again. I was actually very successful with "A Slice of Fear." It's true that it isn't a Stephen King novel and perhaps isn't even close. I seriously doubt that I will sell 100,000 copies of this book, but I can always hope. I'm sure Edgar Allan Poe didn't expect to sell as many books as he did after he was gone, but it happened.

I have become even more fascinated with fear. I know that's hard to believe because I have been fascinated with fears since I was very young, but still, it is something that I look at quite often. Since I wrote "A Slice of Fear," COVID happened, and we got an opportunity to see fear from multiple sides. There were sides looking at losing their lives, sides looking at losing their freedom, and sides that just felt fear for the sake of feeling fear.

As I watched, I was enthralled by the dynamics that I had only read about in books. It is true I have seen fear close up, and I have also felt fear when I was young, but I never saw the level of fear that I saw in the last year and a half.

Although one of the stories in "A Slice of Fear" dealt with COVID it was the last story I added. As I wrote "Another Slice of Fear," I found myself being more brutal and direct with each story. As I did so, I felt I was engaging in more of the nature of fear and less in suspense. You, of course, will be the judge of that. This change in my approach wasn't because I suddenly had the need to be more brutal and direct but instead because it seemed to fit. The world had felt so much fear they were desensitized to it. Depending on which side you were on, you may have been so afraid as to give up your freedom or fight for something that wasn't necessarily true. Either way, in my opinion, you were moving towards living in the shadow of fear. With that in mind I pushed for more intensity, with the sole purpose of dispelling the shadows by darkening them. That creative license creates a larger divide between light and darkness and in itself adds to the suspense of the stories.

The essence of fear is to find that thing inside someone's mind that makes them feel out of control. Fear is knowing that there is nothing you can do that will positively or negatively affect the outcome of a situation, any situation. Fear is something that comes at you so quickly that you act on instinct instead of with intelligence. Fear is deep and lives inside you whether you want it to or not. Those who are brave are not devoid of fear; they have just found a way to deal with it and in the process, overcome their bias of fear and find another path.

When I was young and walking through the woods of Mecosta County in Michigan, I occasionally felt fear in the middle of the night because there were no streetlights, and the true darkness was filled with sounds. I had no idea what was in the darkness, so I felt fear because I could not control it. I often find it funny that now I walk in the dead dark in Muskegon County, Michigan, and know my way without seeing anything. Knowledge dispels fear. Well, usually it does.

As you read, you may find some of the stories more mysterious than fear inciting. You may also find some to be more thrilling, grislier, and more angering. You have to remember; fear is different for everyone. As I sat watching "Annabelle: Creation" in the theater, people screamed and jumped while I giggled. It is different for us all.

One story, "Edges," is a sequel to a story in my book "A Slice of Fear" it stands on its own, but I received numerous requests to take the story forward. So, I did. I hope you enjoy it.

Take a moment and breathe with me, then turn the page and let me spin a few tales that might just take that breath away. I hope you have as much fun reading this little jaunt as I did writing it. I hope you enjoy "Another Slice of Fear."

Immortal

My name is Martin, and I thought I was a scientist until I became something else. My research was exhausting, but I was hopeful that the end result would meet my needs for a long time. I came across the text for a "potion," for lack of a better word, while I was translating ancient Sumerian tablets that had been unearthed in a small city outside of Baghdad.

I employed a series of interns and carefully gave them pieces of text that I knew had no specific meaning to what I was working on. A few simple glyphs in cuneiform nagged at me when I first saw them. It did not take long to realize that the tablet I was working on was a recipe for eternal life.

I am sure that others may have seen the glyphs and realized part of their significance, but I had studied enough of the language that the ingredient list made some sense. What could be translated as the essence of air, I realized, was oxygen and another ingredient, with notes adding fire towards the end of the list, indicating the timing and temperature at which the mixture was to be brewed to make it work. It seemed simple until I got into a series of more complicated glyphs, some I had never seen before. I sat looking at the spiral twists and arrows with no clue how to proceed. The easy parts had been a series of items like cinnamon, turmeric, sage, and basil. It took a little longer to decipher the toxin from the Cerbera Odallam. I was unsure how things that would kill normally would grant eternal life, but I kept trying. After I exhausted all of the common items here, I sat, studying the spirals and text after the Sumerian text, trying to find a key.

It was then I met Gayle. She told me she was twenty-two and had wanted to work with me for some time. Her fiery red hair set her apart from everyone around her, and where most redheads had green or brown eyes, hers were a very light grey with speckles of blue scattered throughout them. She was a graduate student and understood more about Sumerian than any other person I've ever met. After months of working together, we grew close, but I was near fifty, and she was twenty-two, so it was strictly professional. I thought of her as a daughter and couldn't see her as more, no matter what my mind's eye imagined.

After we had worked on the spiral issue together for nearly six months, I threw up my hands. "Why am I wasting my life on a quest only Don Quixote de la Mancha would have undertaken?" ¶Gayle stopped me and looked into my eyes with near pleading intensity.

"Don't you want to find out if it works?"

I looked at those eyes that begged me to continue, and I could do nothing less than walk back with her and keep pushing with all of my being. In only two days, I realized that I had been a fool. Gayle was sitting next to me when I exclaimed, "I've been looking at this all wrong."

"What do you mean?" Gayle asked.

"I have been assuming that this ancient text was written by a primitive man, but I now see that this culture may have been far more advanced than we are today. As I was staring at this twist and the notations, I was also counting, and each of these spiral twists contains twenty-three sequences, and of those sequences, each notation is for a specific count."

"So?" Gayle asked.

"So? Well, if I'm right, then the twenty-three sequences are the twenty-three essential amino acids that are part of our very existence. I think this last notation is a separation of the amino acids to be put inside this 'magic' potion."

"Magic?" Gayle laughed. "This is pure science."

"What is magic but science unexplained? If eternal life isn't magic, I don't know what is." I smiled. "I'm beginning to believe that the essence of all magic may have been based on these texts, and it is as much science as it is magic."

"An interesting theory," Gayle said.

"Knowing what we know now, the sequence is easy, Adenosine, Guanine, and a few others will make up the last ingredients, and we have everything else. Think about it, we know what we need, and we know the proportions from the text. Now it's just a matter of putting it all together."

"What then?" Gayle asked. "Do we release it to the world and let everyone become immortal or don't we? Do we take it and become immortal together forever? What purpose would we have? Have you thought of any of these questions and how this would change everything?"

I pondered for a few moments, not knowing what to say. I was overcome with the knowledge that Gayle and I were at the precipice of discovering; what magic had tried to do for thousands of years. Her questions were good. She was right. I had only thought about the goal but not about the aftermath.

"Gayle," I said, "I am far too old for you."

"If we were immortal what would thirty years mean to 30,000? Could you spend thousands of lifetimes with me, challenged by who I am while becoming more of who you are? Could you love someone that could not die and would be with you for eternity? Could you love me and let me love you in a way beyond what a mortal man could understand?"

I was lost. This young woman asked a series of questions that were literally rocking my world. She walked towards me, and those grey eyes with speckles of blue called my name while she gently kissed my lips. I had never felt so alive.

"I think I could," I heard myself say. "But maybe we should try this 'potion' and then perhaps share it with the world. Think of the changes that man could make with more time. Think of the peace we could create if we eliminated the terror of death."

Gayle's eyes seemed a little sad, but she nodded at me, "We should get to work then."

I was impressed as we began assembling the potion from the instructions translated from the tablet. I was very careful to use handwritten notes and leave very little evidence on computers or anything else for fear of being thought of fool or, worse a charlatan. Gayle was by my side every moment, helping me. She understood more about organic chemistry than anyone I had ever met. At twenty-two, she knew more than the most senior professors. We talked as pieces of the process simmered, and I began to see that the pieces were combining to create more and more unique compounds. It was similar to the process used to create many drugs by using catalyst after catalyst to create a new molecular structure. Gayle agreed, and we ended up in a long discussion about how men and women accused of witchcraft we're actually creating compounds from complex reactions no less impressive than the largest Pharma.

It took nine days to create the formula. Gayle and I grew closer. It felt good as she nuzzled into my neck and kissed me softly, and I knew she was right; she and I could be together forever.

"How should we test this?" she asked.

"I think I should take a dose and see how it works. Then you can take a dose after a week or two, if I survive."

"Why don't you let me take a dose see if it doesn't hurt me?" Gayle countered.

"I just don't want something bad to happen. After all, we have to prove this is safe if we're going to give it to anyone else." I said to her.

"Did you ever see the movie "The Incredibles"?" Gayle asked.

"No, I don't think I did," I replied.

"The bad guy in the movie makes a good point. He built the technology to make everyone super and knew that if everyone was super, no one would be. Giving this formula to the world would be the same. No one would be special, and there would be no fear of death; and as such, no reason to feel the thrill of life."

"That makes sense," I replied. "But don't you think the world would be better if we release this knowledge to everyone?"

"No," Gayle said. "But I have a solution for you for the testing. Let's take it together and either our lives will end, or they will soon begin."

I struggled with that idea but decided this was probably the best choice. If we did this and both of us died, the research would be lost, and no one would take it further. On the other hand, if we both lived, we could decide together, at any time, how to help the world use this fantastic discovery. I explained this to Gayle. She agreed that after we took this potion, we would make the decisions that would guide the world, if we lived.

I admit I was a little apprehensive, but Gayle was so confident. We prepared drinks as was instructed in the tablets. I took all of the research and burned it, knowing that I could recreate it with Gayle in a very short time. I was not worried about the actual tablets as I doubted anyone could understand how I translated them. No one appeared to know as much as she did.

"Are you ready for this?" she asked.

I looked at those beautiful eyes and saw the sparkle. We raised our cups and drank together.

I sat at the table in the center of our lab while Gayle stood, her eyes still sparkling as I felt the pain rush across my body. I tried to move my arms and legs, but I couldn't. I felt weary, and at the same time, I felt a darkness I could not describe.

My vision slowly faded as Gayle held my face and kissed my lips tenderly. I barely felt it, but I was amazed at how passionate and powerful this twenty-two-year-old was in everything she did.

"I'm sorry, Martin. I couldn't let you give eternal life to the world even if it meant that you and I could be together forever. I was so hopeful that you could see the complexity of this formula; how it was more than just some witch's brew and instead, a doorway to forever. You are a good man and good men tend to see the world as a series of good people. I know better. I transposed six of the amino acids knowing they would slowly take the life from you. I'm sorry that you'll have to die, but I have kept this secret safe."

"But you were so young," I tried to stammer weakly.

"It is the good in you that talks to me. I'm not twenty-two years old. I am 22,000 years old and was born in a civilization you called Atlantis. The people there discovered this formula, and we all became immortal. For over 1,000 years, things were good but eventually, the evil of man came out. In the end, I overloaded the reactors and annihilated everyone. You were not reading Sumerian but instead one of its roots." She paused. "I would have loved you like no one ever could have, and we would have been happy together."

"How?" I asked with all my strength.

"I am immortal. No poison affects me."

My eyesight was weakening, and I knew I was dying. The last words I heard were from Gayle, "In another 10,000 years, perhaps I'll find someone who will love me and see the truth."

The Price of Pain

I love the way they scream.

It doesn't take very long for me to get them to the point where they are begging for just another instant of life. I am happy to allow them every additional second, they want until they beg me to die. Then and only then do I take my time and keep them alive as they scream for an end. It is there that I find my happiness, my pleasure, my purpose.

I wasn't always this way. I've always imagined the perfect family life. The white picket fence and coming home to a wonderful wife who would take care of me, and I would spend each day spoiling her. In my senior year of high school, I met Mabel. She was just like any other girl, or so I thought. I couldn't stop looking at her since she was the vision of my dreams. Her dark raven hair was halfway down her back and her grey eyes seemed to speak to me. I was not alone in my feelings. One crisp October afternoon we actually talked.

"I've been watching you," she said. "You watch me all the time."

"I think you're awesome," I replied.

I should have run when she raised an eyebrow, and that wry smile came across her face. Little did I know of the terrors that she had faced. My demise would be my naivete, and my belief that people were basically good.

We started dating, I thought it was pretty normal for the first few weeks. During a long kiss, she suddenly bit me and actually drew blood. As I said "ow" and started to draw back, Mabel held me fast and licked and sucked my lip until the bleeding stopped. She smiled at me. I had no idea the ride I was in for now. After all, I had stayed.

I am not ashamed to say I was a virgin until Mabel. One night as we lay kissing with playful nips and bites, she told me about her life and the horrible things her family had done to her. I was appalled. She told of things that I thought were only in" Special Victims Unit" episodes or some podcast that terrified young men and women in the night. As she told me about the horrors she faced, she began to get excited. I was again unsure of her and felt bad for all she had faced. When I began expressing my sorrow for her, she took my virginity. It was not just an interaction; she took forcible control of me. She was incredibly passionate and near violent the entire time. Even though it was incredible, I knew something was wrong. My life changed forever after that day. She did not stop that night and took me over and over until I had nothing left to give, and then she teased me even further until I pleaded for her to stop. She did not. I was caught between the extreme of wanting it to stop and the intensity of the never-ending moment.

Mabel could not get enough of me after that day. Perhaps six months into our relationship, I found I reveled in every moment with her. It was not just the passion and sex but the constant press for that edge that she gave me. She went far beyond my tolerance levels, and I was in between never wanting it to end and screaming for some sort of respite. Mabel would torture me to the edge of pleasure until there was pain and pleasure as one. I soon realized the pain she could give me had no bounds, and she varied and took me further each time.

Finally, the day came when she showed me how to do the same to her. She was careful, a meticulous teacher. I was a dutiful student and soon, I was doing to her as she had done to me. She began asking me for more and more intensity. I could not resist. Our biting and scratching became razors, light cuts, probes, and more. As the months passed, we experimented more and more. Many times, after we spent hours together, we would lay next to each other dripping fresh blood. It was in those times she was happiest. She was warm and attentive and often fell asleep on me with that wry smile flailing at the edge of my sanity.

We moved in together after dating for seven months. It gave us more time, and we did not fall into the mundane as others would. We had a small house at the end of a cul-de-sac. There we could laugh and scream, and no one was the wiser.

Eight months after I met Mabel, she brought a young woman home. I was confused. The young woman was naïve and curious. Mabel led her to our living room, and we talked for hours. Mabel was toying with the young woman's mind. Mabel was very adept at leading people in conversations, and eventually, she talked about our sex life. It was new for me, and I am sure I was flushed with either excitement or embarrassment. The young woman, Alli, definitely was taken aback. Mabel explained to Alli that the level of enjoyment was based on trust and knowing how far a person could be taken as the line between pain and pleasure blurred. I pondered that for a while as Mabel explained how she and I went to our edges and were lost together. This seemed like an invasion of our privacy, and I felt uncomfortable yet worked up at the same time.

Alli was mesmerized. When Mabel guided her to the bedroom and tied her down, there was no fight.

You have to understand, we had never tied each other, and I was confused. We had no safe words, no special phrase. We just knew where our limits were. We were not always violent, but it was rare for us to have those tender moments that we saw on television or in movies. Instead, we were immersed in passion. We explored each other's pain and pleasure without bounds. Alli was new, and Mabel used a razor to remove her clothes. She grabbed me forcibly, and together we worked on Alli. It was as we had done before, only now we were together with the same goal; to take this young woman to the point where we were often lost, that razor's edge between pleasure and pain.

We spent less than two hours with Alli before she began screaming for us to stop. She had climaxed a dozen times, and her body was racked with both pleasure and pain. Mabel was not interested in stopping. I began seeing this all differently. What was trust between us was now control, and Mabel was in control of both me and Alli. I have to admit, I loved it.

Alli was sobbing and begging for us to stop. Mabel took out a safety pin and pierced her skin. She locked it on Alli and then did so again and again. It was at that point Alli began saying, "No more," quietly. Tears covered her face. Her body was covered in sweat, blood, and a little more. Finally, she passed out on the bed and was silent.

I looked at Mabel. She smiled with that wry smile and took me on the same bed. Alli did not move as we had the best sex we've ever experienced together. Occasionally she would wipe Alli's blood on my lips, and we would revel in the taste and what we had done as we licked and bit each other over and over.

When we rolled over, finally exhausted, we saw that Alli still had not moved. I stood and checked. She was dead, killed by our musings and intensity. Any feeling of remorse was gone when Mabel realized what we had done and became excited all over. Moments later, we were lost in each other again and playing with Alli's body as we pleasured ourselves. We were there for hours and to us, time did not pass at all.

The next day, we wrapped Alli's body and cleaned the house from top to bottom. Alli found her way to the bottom of a quarry bound in chains and wrapped in a garbage bag filled with RidX. Over time, the body would digest, but it was unlikely anyone would trace her to either of us.

Our lives changed to include a new man or woman at least weekly. They were always so into us until it got out of control. Most were like Alli and died of the intensity. It seemed only we could handle the edge of all we created, but one lived. Mabel thought we had found our third.

Her name was Cara, and she was fiery and impulsive and after we took her to the edge of life, she wanted more. Mabel untied her, and the two embraced. This was intensity beyond our imagination. Mabel and I never even considered a third to be possible. I was unsure what was happening until Mabel pulled a knife and plunged it into Cara's stomach. Cara's eyes went wide. Mabel smiled her wry smile and moved back. Cara grabbed the knife, removing it with a scream, and forced it through Mabel's eye socket. The wry smile was gone. Cara fell to the ground gone, and I was alone for the first time in a long time.

I took care of it all. Cara, Mabel, the house, all of it. The house burned to the ground. There would never be evidence again. Now I wander the world and find those people who are looking for more. I find a way to show them what Mabel and I had, and I listen to them scream for mercy until they scream no more. After all, Mabel would want it this way. I will honor her memory by making everyone pay each and every day.

Untouchable

Vladimir disliked his job. Actually, that was not accurate. Vladimir had seething hate for his job. Every moment he was full of angst and worry that he would be caught for the crimes he committed. It's not that his government would prosecute him or that most of his countrymen didn't turn a blind eye to the hack shop that was run in the warehouse. It was that he was not paid well enough for the risks he took.

Vladimir was not a programmer or a hacker. He was a phisher and sat with nearly fifty other men and women calling, emailing, and using Facebook to steal money from the naive and unsuspecting. Today was no different than yesterday, and tomorrow would be the same as the day before yesterday. It was a mundane existence that supported his small apartment and covered the cost of heat during the winter. Most of the people that worked with him were in the same boat. There was no payoff working for their company unless you were a senior programmer, a major hacker, or a whale fisherman. Vladimir wished he could get one payoff from a whale. Those silver-tongued men and women spent days researching a likely C level executive. They sometimes managed to swindle up to $500,000 in a single score.

Krutov, Vladimir's supervisor, started his day telling the entire center that they were not doing enough. Each person in the center was expected to do at least fifty hits per hour. Most of these would turn up dry, but depending on which list you were working, you may get a good Facebook account or a good phone number several times an hour. For phone numbers, you had an opportunity to get one payoff. This was usually a scam involving healthcare or some other nondescript insurance that really didn't exist. It was up to the caller to choose what type of scam they would run based on the voice of the person who answered. If they were older, most callers chose religious or insurance scams. If they were younger, the scam usually had to do with debt for new credit cards. If the scam failed, you simply went on to the next number in your queue. The computers assigned he next available number to you, and when you dialed, it spoofed your outgoing number so you wouldn't get a call back or be traced. Occasionally, you might connect to someone who began a trace outside of the system or who was asking too many questions or playing the line. At that point, you knew it was time to drop, and Vladimir was good at ending those calls.

On this day, Vladimir had been assigned Facebook accounts. The targets were Facebook users who did not add multifactor authentication or whose email and password had been scraped from other areas. Sometimes the hacking group got lucky with the dozens of viruses and ransomware they sent out and picked up user ID's and passwords from computers directly. They monitored those and sent those forward as prime targets. The best accounts to use were the ones that were not used often and would not be recognized. Vladimir was given one of these accounts belonging to Martha Jane Jones and logged on.

As with the phones, his IP was rerouted through a dozen hacked servers or more, If Facebook found him out too quickly, they would not be able to do anything except cut him off, and at that point, his next connection would be scrambled through different servers. The resulting goal was achieved. The group was untouchable.

Martha had over 300 friends. She had been inactive for over three months. Once Vladimir was logged on, he mindlessly reviewed the friend list and finally decided to just start at the beginning. Martha was a seventy-one-year-old woman. Most of her friends were older women and a spattering of older men. The first person he reached out to was not online and did not answer. All he sent was the word "hello." The second person he reached out to answered immediately after he said hello. Vladimir began the process of telling them about this great deal that Martha had found that would supplement Medicare and make certain that bills were paid on time. The woman was very interested in what he was saying, and after a few moments, he sent a link to the site that would begin a process to take money from her. Once the link was sent, he pressed a key on his computer, notifying his supervisor that a link was out, and a light glowed orange above him. Moments later, as he was sending messages to four other people, the light above him glowed green. This meant he had captured a credit card number or a bank account, and the hacking group was in the process of taking what they could from that account before it was detected.

Martha was obviously very popular as he had three more positive hits before things started getting strange. He had been working on the account for nearly forty-five minutes when a reply came back to him, "I heard you died?"

"No, I am still quite alive," Vladimir replied as he spoofed Martha.

"But I'm pretty sure I was at your funeral," the reply came. "It's so hard to remember anymore. Why is it so hard to remember?"

Vladimir was uneasy with this information. He paused and was not typing. Krutov walked up behind him. "Why are you stopping?"

Vladimir pointed to the screen. "This woman may be dead."

"So what," Krutov barked. "You are getting paid for every green light you hit, and you have done very well with this account. You almost covered your whole day in less than an hour. Who cares if she's dead? Ignore that person and move on, obviously, not everyone knew."

Vladimir shook off his nervousness and closed the chat on the confused person. Over the next thirty minutes he got three more good solid credit cards and bank accounts. This made seven total hits on this person, and he was still going strong. Depending upon who was running the finances, this could pay a whole week's salary in a day. Each of the callers worked on commission. Although the supervisors were pointed and terse, they paid well for success.

Vladimir would be paid well for the day. As he progressed, his uneasiness faded, and he thought about the dollars and cents of it all.

Vladimir was not paying attention when he came across the name Terrence Jones. He sent a message to Terrence and said, "hello." He then went on to the next person on Martha's friend list. It was only a few minutes later that he received a message back from Terrence.

"Grandma?" Terrence asked.

Vladimir was not sure which scam to use, so he just said, "Yes."

"Grandma, I've missed you so," Terrence replied. "Are you okay, do you need help?"

Vladimir paused for a moment, and Krutov came up behind him. "What are you waiting for? he has opened the door. Ask for help."

The uneasy feeling was there again, but Vladimir typed out a simple message, "Yes honey, I need your help. Grandma needs money."

The other side of the screen stayed blank. This had worked dozens of times but never with someone who was dead. Vladimir began biting his nails and watching the screen with intensity. Krutov bent down and watched as well, as both of them saw that a reply was being typed.

"I miss you Grandma," was the reply.

"Grandma needs help," Vladimir typed. "Can you send money to me?"

"You are not my grandma," the chat returned. "I am coming for you."

It was Krutov that slammed the red disconnect button on the side of Vladimir's desk. "You have played this account well. We should not push our luck."

On the screen in front of Vladimir he re-read the words, "I am coming for you."

The uneasy feeling was there inside. Vladimir had never had those words said or typed to him before and the thought of being found made him very uneasy. He knew how careful the hackers were, but that didn't make him any less nervous. He knew there was no way to trace him, but that too, his mind ignored. The light above his desk went off, showing that he was not working an account. He looked over to the side on the ninety-five-inch TV and saw that his name was number one today. Based on the numbers to the right of his name, there was no way anyone would catch him. That at least made him feel a little better.

He took a different Facebook account in his queue and began working it. Once again, he was successful, and the green light started coming on again. This person wasn't dead. They had just not taken care of their account, and their friends were gullible, very gullible. When his messenger opened up, Vladimir had six more green lights on this account. Terrence Jones wrote to him, "I'm coming for you."

Vladimir slammed the disconnect button immediately. It was so loud that Krutov came over to him and looked at the screen. "Did you reach out to him?"

"No," Vladimir replied, "I was talking to a woman when the chat window just popped up. He is not even a friend or connected in any way."

Krutov took out his cell phone and dialed a number, "We have a problem. Vladimir appears to have been traced somehow." Krutov hung up the phone. A few minutes later, four men came to the terminal. All of them stared at the message on the screen.

"We have examined the logs already, and Vladimir was not

hacked. There was no connection between Terrence Jones and his new mark. This is inconceivable. Someone identified him without us being able to detect them. Vladimir has done enough today, perhaps enough for the week or even a month. His success today is quite amazing, so perhaps he should take the rest of the day off."

As all of the men turned to the screen for a moment, shaking their heads, the message repeated, "I'm coming for all of you."

There was a murmur for a moment. After pressing the disconnect button, there was no network and no pathway to the screen, but somehow, they watched another message appear where it could not have appeared.

"Vladimir, you go home," Krutov said, "We will take care of this."

As Vladimir stood, the entire center clapped for a moment. Nervously, he looked at the giant screen and saw a star next to his name. He had set a record today. His group had stolen almost $200,000 in his short hour and a half of work. He felt nervous, but he also felt proud. Then he felt ashamed. It was only a moment later that Vladimir felt scared.

He left the warehouse and began walking towards the city and his dingy little apartment. He knew that he would get a very good bonus for today's work, and he thought about moving to someplace nicer. Still, he was haunted by the words he saw on the screen three times today. How could anyone have found him again? How could anyone get around their network? As he walked past the cemetery, he thought of Martha, and he felt ashamed for what he had done. Impersonating a dead woman. This was horrible. What would his mother say? As Vladimir walked, he realized he was lost in his thoughts and almost walked into an older woman. The woman looked up at him and asked if he was okay.

"I am fine," Vladimir said.

"You look like you've seen a ghost young man," the woman

said as she continued on her way.

Vladimir looked into the window next to him and saw a mirror He realized he looked washed out and unsure of himself. He shook it off and continued to walk and knew there was no way they could be traced. Their company was one of the biggest in the world and had almost a billion dollars in revenue from computer crime. They were careful, and that's how they knew everything was safe.

Vladimir reached his apartment and went to the modest room. He turned on his computer and thought about Martha Jane Jones again. He remembered that she was from somewhere in the Midwest and strained his mind to come up with a city. Finally, it came to him, and he looked up Martha Jane Jones in Huntington, West Virginia. There were numerous links, including the Facebook link that would take him to the profile he spoofed today. Instead of going there, he went to the funeral notice on a site called Legacy. He saw a photo of the older woman whom he impersonated. She was a pretty lady even though she was obviously older. She had a glimmer in her eye, even in the picture. He read through the comments posted on the site and saw one from Terrence. All it said was, "I miss you Grandma."

Like all of the employees of their group, his laptop went through an untraceable VPN. Still, Vladimir was nervous about looking up Terrence but did it anyway. Moments later, he was looking at a young a photo of a man of maybe twenty-seven. The young man had a hat on that spoke of guns and guts making America. Vladimir chuckled at the typical American cowboy until his scrolling showed a photo of Terrence in uniform. Terrence was obviously a Marine and based on the medals on his chest, he was a very successful Marine. As he scrolled, he saw numerous posts about the success of Terrence Jones as a sniper and combat instructor. He was also noted as one of the youngest recipients of the Congressional Medal of Honor. Vladimir became even more nervous. Was this someone that they should not have bothered? Should they have done more research? As he clicked one more link, he gasped, it was the obituary for Terrence Jones.

Vladimir was confused and concerned at the same time. As he stared at the obituary, the screen went blank. In a slow scroll, the words filled the screen, "I'm coming for you."

Vladimir closed the laptop and unplugged it. He got up and went to the door, grabbed his jacket, and left his small apartment. His mind was racing as he walked very rapidly back towards the warehouse. Something was wrong, something was very wrong. It was bad enough that this man was a Marine. He heard stories of American Marines decimating troops that were battle-hardened. He always thought it was an exaggeration that the American Marines were killing machines. How could this man be dead and still be talking to him? He did not believe in ghosts, but now his mind was racing, and he was so unsure. Vladimir tripped on the sidewalk and caught himself as he was falling. He saw something out of the corner of his eye. When he looked, nothing was there. Vladimir picked up his pace and saw the warehouse ahead of him. Krutov would know what to do. Someone there would help him.

Vladimir opened the outside door and walked down the hallway to the desk that normally had a guard. No one was there. Vladimir used his keycard and opened the door. It was dark. All he saw was the board with his name still glowing on top. He smelled something. It was like copper. He saw no movement. He reached to his left for the light switch. As he flipped it up, it was sticky. He turned to see pure death. Bodies were strewn everywhere. Krutov was slumped over the top of Vladimir's workstation. His head looked as though it had exploded from within. Bullet holes we're scattered everywhere. He saw people he worked with shot in the face and chest. One of the elite hackers was lying with his eyes wide open and his arm frayed and destroyed as if ripped and torn asunder from his body.

Vladimir heard a small voice and went to a corner. A man he didn't know was crumpled in the corner and coughed. "He said we woke his grandma. He said we had to pay. He said he was coming for us all." At the last word, the man gasped and died. Vladimir turned and grabbed the door, but it was locked now. He scanned the room, and no one was there. Inside he thought of all the bad things he did and all the people that he hurt since he took this job. He looked up at his name with the giant star next to it. He was proud for a moment, but who was left to pay him now?

Vladimir heard a voice, "I found you. You're not my grandma."

"I'm sorry," Vladimir screamed. "Please, I'm sorry."

Vladimir saw the single red dot light up his chest. He looked around the room but there was nothing there. Then, he saw a flash, and as he looked down, there was a hole where his heart used to be.

As his vision faded, he heard a voice that he had never heard before, "I miss you Grandma." A young man standing over him faded from his view. It was the last thing Vladimir saw as he slipped into death and the hell that waited.

Drained

Alison awoke in a panic. She realized she was tied down and could not move. She wrenched her hands back and forth but saw them bound with a thick rope and tight knots. Allison kicked her legs from side to side to no avail. They, too, were held fast. She realized she was on a gurney or rolling table from the slight movements that jiggled as she struggled.

"Hello!" Allison screamed. "Why am I here?" Allison kicked again. Nothing happened. She pulled hard on her arms and strained against the ropes until she felt them cutting into her skin. "Hello!"

A door opened in the distance, and Alison heard the *click* of shoes against concrete pavement. The steps got closer.   She wondered who tied her down.

The last thing Alison remembered was being at a bar having a quick drink with her friend Monica before she went home. She strained to remember. She realized that Monica left first, and as she paid the tab, a handsome young man offered to buy her a drink. She remembered he was so accommodating and kept touching her side. The last thing that she clearly remembered was the bug bite on her neck.

"Nice to see you awake," a deep voice said. "I was worried you would sleep through the fun."

"Who?" Alison asked.

"We will get to that," the voice replied as she heard the scooting of steel against concrete. She saw an older man, perhaps fifty, with wire-rim glasses in a dress shirt. He looked crisp and professional. His hair was parted and clean, his eyes were dark brown or grey, she could not tell. His hair was grey speckles inside of brown.

"Who are you?" Alison asked again.

"Call me Dad," the man said. "It will make sense in a while. I am sorry I had to get you here this way. I would have rather met you and talked, but you were having none of that. How many messages have I left for you on your phone asking you to talk to me?"

"How should I know," Alison's indignance was palpable. "I have no fucking idea who you are."

"Oh, I see," the man said, "You kill a lot of people."

"I have never killed anyone!" Alison spat.

"My son would disagree if he was still alive," the man said. "You sucked the life right out of him and didn't even care when he died. Have you forgotten him already?"

A glimmer of recognition sparked in Alison's eyes. "Are you Jay's father?"

"Ahh," the man said. "See, now we are getting somewhere."

"I didn't kill your son," Alison pleaded. "Jay was not himself, he overdid, and I just couldn't take it anymore."

"Funny," the man interrupted. "I have his diary and the tapes he kept of his daily walks. It is actually quite a story. It would make a good Hallmark show up until the end. No, no, it does not end like Hallmark would. Jay worked hard to give you everything you wanted and then came home to you with another man. He gave you everything, and you took everything. There was little left of him when he left. Remember how he just walked away from you? He let you have all his hard work, his house, his life, all of it. I was so sad when he came home, distraught. He just wasted away. He wouldn't eat or sleep, or really engage at all. He just kept saying, 'Love was not enough,' and how much he still loved you. I called you over and over. A kind word would have saved him. A moment with you may have opened his mind to something more, but you wouldn't talk to me. You didn't even come to the funeral. You just went to the lawyers, pulled the house out of his name, made it all yours."

Alison was crying a little, "I did love Jay; it is just he was never there, he worked so much, and I was lonely."

Again, the man interrupted her, "Oh yes, I know all about his work ethic. My fault, I suppose. I spent far too much time working and could have done more. Still, I did spend a lot of time with him growing up, and every day with him until he died, after he came home. It was so sad seeing him waste away, knowing I could not fix it. With all my amazing toys, there was no making it better."

"Why am I here? Are you going to kill me?" Alison said.

"Oh, that would be too easy," the man replied. "I want you to understand how poorly my Jay felt. I want you to know the despair that plagued him during his last days. Let me show you something."

The lights came on. A bright steel chair was illuminated on the far side of the room. The clamps and stirrups on it looked cold and formidable. Next to the chair was half of a human body. A woman with a robotic torso and base. Her face was pretty. Blonde hair flowed under her nurse's cap. Her top half wore a nurse's uniform over her proportioned shape.

"Hot robot," Alison sprayed. "You a pervert too?"

"No, I am just a bit of an inventor. I have two of my creations that will be taking care of you. I wanted to introduce you to Momma first. She will make sure you live. Anything necessary, she will give you. She'll make sure you survive. She can even talk to you, interact, and keep you in near-perfect health. The chair is built for your comfort. I spent a lot of time on the pieces in the torso; no infections to come, no itchy parts. The waste removal system is quite amazing. NASA is now looking at it as a replacement for their current systems. Your comfort and your health were my primary concerns."

"What's the catch," Alison asked.

"Well, you met b0b but allow me to reintroduce you." The man waved. Alison could not see, but now heard something buzz around her. She saw it land on her chest. It looked like a small fly, but she could see it was shiny, like brushed chrome or steel. She focused and saw the bug-like robot move around, watching her, with a tiny glowing eye.

"Is that what stung me?" Alison asked.

"Well," the man began, "it did not sting you. It injected you with a toxin that eliminated your memory and struggles. Then it returned to me as I came into the building to usher you to the car. You were very prone to suggestions, and it looked like I saved you from date rape. b0b was just doing his job, but he only has a few hundred gigabytes of storage. I didn't program him to wait 'til your suitor left. b0b can also remove blood and sample DNA, and even process a lot from the data it receives.

"Why?" Alison asked.

"Why?" the man asked. "You are a smart, conniving woman Alison. I am surprised you haven't figured it out yet, but some of this will be a little above your head. You will have two companions for the rest of your life. Momma, who will spend her programming cycles to save you, and my little friend and his pals who will be doing as you did to Jay, sucking the life out of you."

"What?" Alison barked.

"Yes," the man said. "Show her."

The minuscule robot walked with an almost superior shuffle from Alison's sheet to her exposed arm. Once there, the robot pushed a small needle into her arm. Alison could see the back area filling dark red. It was almost like a mosquito as it filled, and a short few seconds later, the little robot stopped, then flew away.

"Your little robot is going to take my blood?" Alison asked.

"Yes," the man replied. "b0b will take your blood and transfer it to the repository. Once that is done, he will return and take more.

As you grow closer to death, Momma will feed you and help you survive. As your blood level decreases, you will feel drained further and further until you can no longer easily function. At that point, b0b will stop and recharge while Momma gets you back to 100%, then we will start again. I figure after the twentieth time, you will perhaps appreciate how my son felt."

"Someone will find me!" Alison was defiant still.

"No, you are in an underground bunker. There is no trace, no way in or out except via a cave, and no easy way there. You will be here for the rest of your life. Perhaps twenty or thirty years. You should be a little impressed. I put so much time into making this perfect for you."

"Fuck you," Alison seethed.

"Put her to sleep b0b," the man said.

Alison awoke a short time later. She was in the chair now, comfortable except for her nervousness. But she was aware she was held down. She was now wearing a hospital gown, yet exposed underneath. She felt a softness near her torso and knew the waste removal system was there.

"We will be such great friends," the robot named Momma said.

"Have a life," the man said as he walked into view.

"Your one little bug will take forever to bother me. I will get out," Alison stated.

"I know I have been calling him b0b and you hear that as 'b-o-b'. His real name is B zero B. Are you familiar with hexadecimal? If so, you would know B zero B is 2827. That is his designation. He has brothers, you see. Here they come now."

Alison saw the cloud flying towards her and was wide-eyed. Her bravado gone, all she could do was scream as 2,827 tiny needles penetrated her body. As the room began to spin she heard the *click* of shoes leaving and wondered if this was how Jay felt: Alone in the dark with no hope.

The Boathouse

The three stories that follow were part of a weird idea that floated around in my head. Each is the same in one way describing a situation from a very different point of view. I have always found it amazing how ineffective we are at seeing other points of view. These stories suggest an even wider chasm in understanding.

Andrew

The waves lapped against the shoreline with a consistent rhythmic *thrum* from the water hitting the bottom of the boathouse. It was situated about 150 feet out into the pier. Kate walked next to me with her inquisitive and cautious attitude. The two played against each other as people were rarely inquisitive and cautious. I knew how special Kate was, and it was imperative I get her to the boathouse.

"It's this way," I said. "Out here by the boathouse. This will be the most amazing writing prompt you have ever experienced."

Kate eyed me suspiciously. "Why didn't you bring it to me? All this cloak and dagger, and leading me out here alone? You always concern me, Andrew but never as much as today."

"You know me," I said. "Always a flair for the dramatic."

"That's what worries me," Kate laughed with a nervous quiver few would detect. "This is the ocean. It has sharks. You know how I feel about sharks."

"Yes, I know how you feel about sharks, and yes, I know that the ocean isn't exactly your favorite, but I think this writing prompt will vault you to new heights. I can honestly say that you'll be tied up in it for a long time and never want to get out."

"That's not much better," Kate laughed. "I know you're very

careful about your word choices in just about everything you do, and your word choice right now is a little concerning."

"Would it help if I promised you that you will be 100% safe from sharks," I laughed.

"Not really, no," Kate laughed with me for a moment. "I would feel a whole lot better four miles inside the coastline, not having to think about waves and all the things underneath them."

"Again, I promise you there is nothing to fear in or beneath the water here." I was as earnest as I could be.

"Are you sure this pier is safe?" Kate asked, still hesitating.

"I've been out here several times doing my own research, but I think this will open you up to new possibilities," I said.

"You've said that several times. I am intrigued and cautious," Kate said. "Still, it's not going to hurt to take a walk and just see what you're talking about."

"You'll have to see it to believe it," I said, "and even then, I'm not sure you'll fully grasp the beauty of what I'm about to show you."

"Well, Mr. Smith," Kate smiled, "if I didn't know better, I would say you're trying to seduce me."

"Me?" I laughed. "No, I am not. I wouldn't do that to you."

"That at least makes me feel a little better." Kate smiled as we began carefully walking the pier. "You are usually difficult to read, even though I have excessive experience reading people and determining their motivations so I can teach them more effectively. You wear many layers of complexity. It is always hard to tell when you are serious."

"If you had lived my life, you would be covered in layers as well," I stated. "We've both had difficult lives, but mine has more depth than most could consider. Because of the harshness of my childhood and constant negative reinforcement, my positive nature was built on hardened ground." We were now about thirty feet from the boathouse. "It makes it difficult for people to see past what I show them. Even when I write, there are layers upon layers of subplots, and many will never be seen by the reader until they reread and reread again."

"I can't believe you talked me into this," Kate said as she looked at the waves still lapping at the boathouse and pier. "How deep is the water here?"

"Where we're at now is about fifty feet, maybe a little more. You don't have to worry, though; these posts are driven deep, and there is no way this pier will fall."

Kate looked over the edge of the pier with a caution that only a few would understand. The murky depths beckoned below, yet nothing moved. We were now at the boathouse. I opened the pristine door to the darkness inside.

"Is there a light?" Kate asked. "Can I even see this thing you want me to see?"

"This is gravy," I said. "I want you to be able to explain this to Diana because she'll want to be a part of this as well. Maybe tell me how to explain it, and I'll go get her while you get tied up in your writing." I stepped inside, in front of her, and walked towards the back. There was light from the ocean where two large boats lay in their slips but did not go far beneath the water. Tools and gas cans littered the area, as well as nets and other items. My eyes adjusted to the light easily as they had many times. Kate timidly followed me, and the door silently closed behind her. She did not notice as she was looking at the sight before her.

It would be difficult to explain to someone who had never seen a shark up close. There, in the corner of the boathouse, was the carcass of a shark. It was held by filaments affixed to multiple areas of the wall. Hundreds and hundreds of fine filaments made up a net that was far more intricate than a snowflake under a microscope.

"What in the world?" Kate said, "How did you find this, and what in the world got it up here?"

"Funny you should ask," I said. "I found this place completely by accident as I was taking pictures. I knew it was a perfect place to fish and, well, what I found was fascinating. The shark is a bonus. It is not what we are here to see."

Now on guard, Kate began to look around and noticed the door was closed. She started to walk to it and noticed something else above the door, patiently waiting for her.

"Hellooo Kaaate," the raspy voice hissed. "Aaandrew has toold me soo much about you."

From above, it slowly lowered itself to the floor. The eight legs stood almost four feet tall, and the body was nearly as large as a small boat. Kate stepped back and fell into me. I held her arms and caught her. She turned into me and looked up into my eyes with a combination of terror, curiosity, and something else. She turned back around and looked into the eight eyes staring at the two of us and then noted the chelicerae with very small fangs for a creature this size.

"Why did you bring me here?" Kate asked. "How can this thing talk?"

"She's not a thing," I said. "Chrylsla is very old, and she just wants to talk."

"Is that why you had to trick me to get me here?" Kate sneered.

"Wouldst thou have come if heee had askkked?" Chrylsla queried.

Kate turned to the creature. "Probably not, but I would have considered it. It wouldn't be a lie, at least."

"Then thou hast annnswered thy question," Chrylsla said. "I asssked Andreew to bring me more knowledge, and someone to once again test for forever. He hast chosen thou."

"Really?" Kates said and snapped back to look at me. "So, what am I supposed to be, some type of walking encyclopedia or a magnificent chew toy?" I laughed at the way she kept some control in this situation. She was perfect.

"Something like that," I said. "She is looking for knowledge about her kind. I have given her all that I can and have been researching on the Internet for any other similar creature, but to no avail. I have access to significantly more information than most people are aware. Still, even I have found no mention of a creature like this."

"What do you mean you have access to more information?" Kate asked me.

I struggled for just a moment trying to decide how to approach this question. It had always come to this, and always I tried to come up with a reasonable statement. Usually no one listened. "Well, I actually started researching this about 250 years ago." Kate looked incredulously at me and smirked for just a moment. "Don't smirk and just listen for a moment," I said while gesturing for her to calm down. Thinking about it now, I've realized that telling anyone to calm down is likely the wrong thing to do. Telling someone to calm down when they are a woman, a writer, have seen a shark in a giant spider's web in the last ten minutes, have seen an 800-pound spider in the last seven minutes, while you're telling them that you're about 275 years old isn't going to get a calm reaction. "Kate, I came over on a British ship in 1773. I was wandering the beaches and found a cave. Inside was Chrylsla. She was hungry for knowledge and just plain hungry, so I started fishing for her as she couldn't leave the cave back then. I could have run, but I decided not to. Over time, I found she could learn my language, and in the process, we communicated."

"That really doesn't explain anything," Kate said. "275 years old, really?"

"Somewhere in the middle of it she bit me," I said. "When she did, I found out that it reacted with my blood and almost completely eliminated disease and the aging process. I have tested the theory in a lab. My blood is immune to everything now."

"She bit you?" Kate was getting furious. "You let this thing bite you?"

"Enouuuugh of thissss," Chrylsla crackled. I knew she was getting impatient, and I knew it was time.

"Kate, I like you, but I have to do this just to find out if there's someone else like me." I grabbed Kate by one arm, and as she swung at me with her other, I grabbed it as well. I towered over her and was many times stronger than her. "This might be the start of a new life for you. Imagine all you can do."

Kate screamed at the top of her lungs. It was more from frustration and anger than it was from any type of fear. "Damn you," she spat as she tried to struggle. Chrylsla moved up behind her, and one of her legs reached out to Kate's shoulder. I could see the poison gather on Chrylsla's fangs.

The boathouse started shaking slightly, and several of the trigger wires in the water began moving rapidly. Chrylsla looked to the water. "Ittt is a larggeee one of the teeth." Without warning, a great white shark jumped from the water into the boathouse, grabbing the hanging shark above it. It only took a moment for the shark to tangle in the complexly woven web. Chrylsla rushed forward, but this shark was much larger and snapped the cabled spider silk, and a part of boathouse along with it. I turned to see Kate push by and slam through the door onto the pier. She took something with her that I couldn't see. As Chrylsla and I struggled with the shark, I saw the flames. Kate had taken a gas can and set the boathouse on fire. Chrylsla looked around and then to me, chittering.

"Into the boat," I said, and Chrylsla and I boarded the twenty-eight-foot cruiser. I fired up the engines and pushed the throttle forward as the huge shark fell into the water behind us. The boat slammed into the overhead door and out into the sunlight as Chrylsla went below deck. Through the flames, I saw Kate as we moved into the open ocean, running to the beach and her waiting car. She knows we are out here now, and we will find her. We have no choice.

Chrylsla

The pain seemed to never end. I could set it aside, but it was insistent and had been for so many turns of the sky. The waves lapped against the shoreline with a rhythmic *thrum* as the water hit the bottom of the structure. I was not happy with this "thinkers of the warm blood" structure, but the man thought it helped. I looked at the "water of the large teeth" in my snare. It would not be able to be eaten for much longer as the smell of death was now overpowering.

I tried to relax in the nest I made in the corner. The fine silk was strong. It had served me well for uncounted turns of the sun and could hold against even the most fearsome creature of the teeth. I remembered the giant creatures of old who fought with the "forever seers of the light" like I, and how many teeth they tried to use to no result. That was when we were many. Now, I may be the last. The eggs that I carry each cannot be completed, and as they fail, my system aches and hurts until they can be expelled or reabsorbed into my body. If I found a mate, the pain would be gone. I have not mated since we created the first thinkers of the warm blood.

I heard the male who calls himself Andrew in the distance. The threads to me send the vibrations, and I know he is coming. Perhaps with another who is more pure and can open their mind and frail body to forever. I am amused at how the first thinkers of the warm blood would have lived as long as I, but they mated with those that were not given our venom and became weak and of short life. The nature of the thinkers of the warm blood was their undoing. The war that came killed most of the pure and many of the forever seers of the light. We were scattered and used stealth to live. We kept some of the thinkers of the warm blood who survived with us. My last left for food in the time of the great ice and never returned. Each time I tried to help another become more, they did not survive, until Andrew.

I heard them outside and curled so I would not startle the

new thinker of the warm blood. Andrew was certain she would be able to open her mind and her life, and was of the intelligence to help us, to help me. I made myself not seen at the top of the structure and waited. I heard them speak, their language was simple, but it was difficult for me to make the sounds or imitate as they did.

"It's this way," Andrew said. "Out here by the boathouse. This will be the most amazing writing prompt you have ever experienced."

"Why didn't you bring it to me? All this cloak and dagger, and leading me out here alone? You always concern me, Andrew but never as much as today."

"You know me," Andrew said "Always a flair for the dramatic."

"That's what worries me," the other said. "This is the ocean. It has sharks. You know how I feel about sharks."

"Yes, I know how you feel about sharks, and yes, I know that the ocean isn't exactly your favorite, but I think this writing prompt will vault you to new heights. I can honestly say that you'll be tied up in it for a long time and never want to get out," Andrew said. His words concerned me as they baited the other.

"That's not much better," she stated. "I know you're very careful about your word choices in just about everything you do, and your word choice right now is a little concerning."

"Would it help if I promised you that you will be 100% safe from sharks?" Andrew replied.

"Not really, no," the other said. "I would feel a whole lot better four miles inside the coastline, not having to think about waves and all the things underneath them."

"Again, I promise you there is nothing to fear in or beneath the water here," Andrew replied.

"Are you sure this pier is safe?" I heard her words but knew she was cautious.

"I've been out here several times doing my own research, but I think this will open you up to new possibilities," Andrew tried to comfort the other.

Their words continued, but the pain held me again. This time, it was hard. If only I could explain to Andrew how to relieve the pressure. I did not have the words, and he thought it a pang of hunger for hundreds of years. I needed another to try to explain the process.

The door opened, and Andrew passed through. I waited.

"Is there a light?" the other asked. "Can I even see this thing you want me to see?"

"This is gravy," Andrew said. "I want you to be able to explain this to Diana because she'll want to be a part of this as well. Maybe tell me how to explain it, and I'll go get her while you get tied up in your writing." She passed under me, looking at our previous kill. I waited, hoping this would be a start to finding a way to live without the pain or find a mate.

"What in the world?" the female was mystified. "How did you find this, and what in the world got it up here?"

"Funny you should ask," Andrew said. "I found this place completely by accident as I was taking pictures. I knew it was a perfect place to fish and, well, what I found was fascinating. The shark is a bonus. It is not what we are here to see."

I lowered to the ground and closed the door behind the other.

"Hellooo Kaaate," I put in their words. "Aaandrew has toold me soo much about you."

I stood and saw her recoil. I knew of their fear. I waited.

"Why did you bring me here?" she asked. "How can this thing

talk?"

"She's not a thing," Andrew said. "Chrylsla is very old, and she just wants to talk." His thoughts for me had grown. It was good.

"Is that why you had to trick me to get me here?" I heard the other say.

"Wouldst thou have come if heee had askkked?" I queried.

She turned, "Probably not, but I would have considered it. It wouldn't be a lie, at least."

"Then thou hast annnswered thy question," I said. "I asssked Andreew to bring me more knowledge and someone to once again test for forever. He hast chosen thou."

"Really?" she said, "So what am I supposed to be, some type of walking encyclopedia or a magnificent chew toy?"

"Something like that," Andrew said. "She is looking for knowledge about her kind. I have given her all that I can and have been researching on the Internet for any other similar creature, but to no avail. I have access to significantly more information than most people are aware of, but even I have found no mention of a creature like this."

"What do you mean you have access to more information?" Kate asked in a different tone.

"Well, I actually started researching this about 250 years ago. Don't smirk and just listen for a moment," Andrew said while gesturing. He continued, "Kate, I came over on a British ship in 1773. I was wandering the beaches and found a cave. Inside was Chrylsla. She was hungry for knowledge and just plain hungry, so I started fishing for her, as she couldn't leave the cave back then. I could have run, but I decided not to. Over time, I found she could learn my language, and in the process, we communicated."

"That really doesn't explain anything," Kate said with

curiosity. "275 years old, really?"

"Somewhere in the middle of it, she bit me," Andrew said. "When she did, I found out that it reacted with my blood, eliminating disease and much of the aging process. I have tested the theory in a lab. My blood is immune to everything now."

"She bit you?" Kate was angered. "You let this thing bite you?"

Our kind had set theirs in motion. They owed us more than they knew. Always this thought of selfish needs. All I needed was to stop the pain. I felt the mind of the furious one come upon me. "Enouuuugh of thissss," I forced in their sounds, in their words.

"Kate, I like you, but I have to do this just to find out if there's someone else like me." Andrew grabbed her and controlled her. "This might be the start of a new life for you."

Kate screamed at the top of her lungs. "Damn you," she was not in control. I came to her. Perhaps this would be the start of new life and less pain.

I was deceived. My snare silk started moving rapidly. I looked at the water. "Ittt is a larggeee one of the teeth." It was the mate of the other, back again for fury. Their kind was relentless when focused. I had to stop it, fast. It only took a moment for the water of the teeth to tangle in my snare. I rushed forward, but it snapped the snare and the structure. I saw the one Andrew called Kate run from the room with the fire liquid. I was concerned. I saw the flame around the boathouse. We had been deceived. It would consume the structure in a short time. Andrew was resilient and intelligent for his kind, he guided me to the hold in the water, and I went below in the dark. I felt the thing he called engine whine, and we were moving. Then an impact, and we were in the open water, away from the place.

I know this one named Kate has the cunning to be close to the pure and perhaps survive. We must find her, and perhaps she will be able to help stop the pain. Perhaps she will help find my own kind so I can again mate. Perhaps, but for now, Andrew must find us another roost, and we will work together to feed. I do not want to die, so I will fight for my life and keep going.

Kate

The waves lapped against the shoreline with a rhythmic *thrum* as the water hit the bottom of the boathouse. It was situated about 150 feet out into the pier. Andrew walked next to me with his usual confident attitude. His stride was measured, but there was something almost comical about his walk. Andrew was different from most. Though I was not sure of his training, it was there. I was always both cautious and curious about my interactions with him.

"It's this way," Andrew said. "Out here by the boathouse. This will be the most amazing writing prompt you have ever experienced."

I was weary. My senses were tingling in many ways. "Why didn't you bring it to me? All this cloak and dagger, and leading me out here alone? You always concern me, Andrew but never as much as today."

"You know me," he said. "Always a flair for the dramatic."

"That's what worries me," I laughed, hoping he would not sense my caution. "This is the ocean. It has sharks. You know how I feel about sharks." I hate sharks. Well, I used to hate them.

"Yes, I know how you feel about sharks, and yes, I know that the ocean isn't exactly your favorite, but I think this writing prompt will vault you to new heights. I can honestly say that you'll be tied up in it for a long time and never want to get out." Andrew was being positive, but there was something in his words, his voice.

"That's not much better," I laughed while surveying the area. "I know you're very careful about your word choices in just about everything you do, and your word choice right now is a little concerning." The area was clear, but I knew that already.

"Would it help if I promised you that you will be 100% safe from sharks?"

"Not really, no," I considered. "I would feel a whole lot better four miles inside the coastline, not having to think about waves and all the things underneath them."

"Again, I promise you there is nothing to fear in or beneath the water here," Andrew stated dryly.

"Are you sure this pier is safe?" I stalled.

"I've been out here several times doing my own research, but I think this will open you up to new possibilities," Andrew replied.

"You've said that several times. I am intrigued and cautious." I had come this far; I had to face this fear. "Still, it's not going to hurt to take a walk and just see what you're talking about."

"You'll have to see it to believe it," Andrew said, "and even then, I'm not sure you'll fully grasp the beauty of what I'm about to show you."

"Well, Mr. Smith," I was again suspicious, "if I didn't know better, I would say you're trying to seduce me."

"Me?" Andrew laughed. "No, I am not. I wouldn't do that to you."

"That at least makes me feel a little better." I knew he was lying. He wanted something. "You are usually difficult to read, even though I have excessive experience reading people, and determining their motivations so I can teach them more effectively. You wear many layers of complexity. It is always hard to tell when you are serious."

"If you had lived my life, you would be covered in layers, as well," Andrew replied. "We've both had difficult lives, but mine has more depth than most could consider. Because of the harshness of my childhood and constant negative reinforcement, my positive nature was built on hardened ground. It makes it difficult for people to see past what I show them. Even when I write, there are layers upon layers of subplots, and many will never be seen by the reader until they reread and reread again."

"I can't believe you talked me into this," I said as I realized the gravity of my situation. "How deep is the water here?"

"Where we're at now is about fifty feet, maybe a little more. You don't have to worry, though; these posts are driven deep, and there is no way this pier will fall."

I looked over the pier's edge, searching for a trap, yet saw none. We were now at the boathouse, and Andrew opened the pristine door to the darkness inside.

"Is there a light?" I asked. "Can I even see this thing you want me to see?"

"This is gravy," Andrew said. "I want you to be able to explain this to Diana because she'll want to be a part of this as well. Maybe tell me how to explain it, and I'll go get her while you get tied up in your writing." He walked in, and I followed. There was dim light where two large boats lay in their slips. The doors did not go far beneath the water. The area was cluttered, and I made a note of anything I might need. My eyes adjusted to the light slowly, but I followed him. Then I saw it. There, in the corner of the boathouse was the carcass of a shark. It was held by filaments affixed to multiple areas of the wall. Hundreds and hundreds of fine filaments made up a mesh that looked as strong as steel. It had to be. I gauged the fish at over 400 pounds.

"What in the world?" I was mystified, "How did you find this, and what in the world got it up here?"

"Funny you should ask," Andrew said. "I found this place completely by accident as I was taking pictures. I knew it was a perfect place to fish and, well, what I found was fascinating. The shark is a bonus. It is not what we are here to see."

I had been a fool. Something was very wrong. I had minimal

weapons and no advantage. I had to play the game now until I had an opening. I turned to leave, and then I saw it, a shadow above the door. I froze.

"Hellooo Kaaate," the raspy voice hissed. "Aaandrew has toold me soo much about you."

From above, it slowly lowered itself to the floor. The eight legs stood almost four feet tall, and the body was nearly as large as a small boat. I stepped back into Andrew. He grabbed me. I turned, looking up into his eyes. I had to find my opening now. This was nothing I was trained for; I was patient. It would come. I turned around and looked into the eight eyes staring at me and noted the fangs.

"Why did you bring me here?" I asked. "How can this thing talk?" I was stalling but curious as well.

"She's not a thing," Andrew said "Chrylsla is very old, and she just wants to talk."

"Is that why you had to trick me to get me here?" I sneered, checking the area for anything I could use.

"Wouldst thou have come if heee had askkked?" Chrylsla queried.

I turned, "Probably not, but I would have considered it. It wouldn't be a lie, at least."

"Then thou hast annnswered thy question," Chrylsla said. "I asssked Andreew to bring me more knowledge and someone to once again test for forever. He hast chosen thou."

"Really?" I said. "So what am I supposed to be, some type of walking encyclopedia or a magnificent chew toy?" I saw something move in the water.

"Something like that," Andrew said. "She is looking for knowledge about her kind. I have given her all that I can, and I have been researching on the Internet for any other similar creature, but to no avail. I have access to significantly more information than most people are aware of, but even I have found no mention of a creature like this."

"What do you mean you have access to more information?" I asked. He seemed stunned that I would question him. He paused, looked confused, then continued.

"Well, I actually started researching this about 250 years ago. Don't smirk and just listen for a moment," he said, while gesturing for me to calm down.

Calm down? Calm down? If I had my M9, I would have shot him and the creature with him just for suggesting something so stupid. Imagine asking me to calm down while explaining I might be lunch.

He continued, "Kate, I came over on a British ship in 1773. I was wandering the beaches and found a cave. Inside was Chrylsla. She was hungry for knowledge and just plain hungry, so I started fishing for her, as she couldn't leave the cave back then. I could have run, but I decided not to. Over time, I found she could learn my language, and in the process, we communicated."

"That really doesn't explain anything," I said, not wanting to show my fascination. "275 years old, really?"

"Somewhere in the middle of it, she bit me," Andrew said. "When she did, I found out that it reacted with my blood and nearly eliminated disease and the aging process. I have tested the theory in a lab. My blood is immune to everything now."

"She bit you?" I was even more furious. I was on the menu, and I was not going down like a lobster in a pot. I was fighting my way out. "You let this thing bite you?"

"Enouuuugh of thissss," Chrylsla crackled. I knew I was in trouble. The giant Charlotte was hungry.

"Kate, I like you, but I have to do this just to find out if there's someone else like me." Andrew grabbed me by one arm, and as I swung at him with my other, he grabbed it as well. I had never underestimated someone so much. I was trapped, unable to gain purchase, and he was many times stronger than I. "This might be the start of a new life for you." He smiled. I imagined removing his smile with a dull knife and felt better.

I screamed at the top of my lungs. I was mad. No, I was furious. "Damn you," I spat and fought as hard as I could, seeing the water move again with my fury. I could feel the creepy crawler behind me and knew this might be the end.

I saw the movement in the water again and struggled more. The boathouse started shaking slightly, and several of the trigger wires began moving rapidly in the water. Chrylsla looked to the water. "Ittt is a larggeee one of the teeth." Without warning, a great white shark jumped from the water into the boathouse, grabbing the hanging shark above it. It only took a moment for the shark to tangle in the complexly woven web. Chrylsla rushed forward, but this shark was much larger and snapped the cabled spider silk and also part of boathouse. This was my chance. I grabbed two cans on the ground and felt them slosh. I ran to the door and crashed onto the pier. Dropping to my knees, I sprayed the contents of the cans onto the boathouse and pier, then reached into my pocket for a match. I knew I had one, and it lit easily. The fire took off, and I ran hard to the dock.

The fire was high and burned fast. I wondered if Andrew or the spider would survive. Then I saw the larger of the two boats slam out of the boathouse and head out to sea. I ran to the beach, hoping I could get my M9 and squeeze off a few shots, but it was too far. I watched as the boat disappeared into the horizon. I know they are out there now, and I will find them. I will track them to the end of the world if necessary. It will not end well for them, or perhaps for me, but it will end.

Monster

I survived. It had been untold millennia since I was, and it will be untold millennia before I am no more. I have struck terror into nearly every creature that has ever been on this world. I have been the stuff of legends and far more. I have thought for thousands of years that I have lived so long because even death is afraid of me. I see death often. Even his shadow cannot hide from my watchful eye.

Somewhere in the midst of it all, I found myself in this Side Show. I sit in my cage with reinforced bars of the metal the humans call steel and wander through the days. I am not truly a prisoner but instead am imprisoned by my thoughts and held captive by so many that have gone before me. In cages around me are numerous creatures that have survived or hidden during the human age.

Two pixies are in a cage near me, and their incessant buzzing is often annoying. When I look their way, they are silent as they remember the time long ago when I nearly destroyed them all for their annoyance. I look to them with sadness now, for all they ever wanted to do was find a way to make me smile.

Near the pixies is a baby dragon. It has not grown since I have been here, and I fear it is stunted and will be a prisoner for many of its long years. Sometimes the dragon sings, and I am reminded of a time when dragons were scattered across the sky. Their songs were beautiful and told the stories of the 10,000 years that they ruled the world. That time was gone in the blink of my eye, and I had not seen another dragon until I came here.

In another cage, there is a misshapen unicorn. Her near-perfect horn sits upon a body that seems to be racked with pain. I can see that either her legs had formed wrong, or they were broken at a young age and never healed properly. She stumbles in the cage but does not give up. She is proud to be alive.

There are dozens of other cages and each holds something I

know of or something I had thought long since gone. All of them fear me, for many know the stories of my rage and the tales of my past. I have many names given to me by the creatures of this planet. All of them can be summed up in one human word: monster. I am not burdened by a fear of death nor a fear of life. I am not burdened by fear. Instead, I am the harbinger of doom when I find something in my path. For untold eons, I simply walked the planet, eliminating anything that I wanted without regard to the past, present, or future.

The humans are almost unique. They rose only a short time ago to make themselves the masters of the world. I saw them when they threw simple spears and rocks and simply walked away, not willing to lay waste to another species. By that time, I tired of death and the constant annoyance of causing it. I was and am tired. The human languages are simple, and their minds even more simple. The pixies, for example, have a complex language rooted in the mathematical process of the sun. They can communicate great amounts in a very short time with tremendous meaning. The dragons communicate by song, and many of the great old dragons lived long enough that they no longer feared me and instead sang to me of my many adventures, of my facing the giants of the age, and resetting the sea to stop the great monsters of the deep. The old dragons were wise and nearly fearless. The young dragon before me barely sings and seems beaten down by captivity. Someday the dragons may rise again as they have several times. Their long cycles in the egg are well beyond the existence of humans.

I could not tell you how long I have been imprisoned by the one called Marlow. I was sleeping, and he and a group put me in this cage and brought me here. They cannot harm me, nor can they possibly understand what I am. It seems like only a moment, for what is time to me when I have nothing but time? Marlow sells tickets for other humans to gawk and cringe in terror at my visage. I have not left simply because I have nowhere else to go. It is enough to be amused by the interactions of the humans. I stay and am as I have become, full of apathy and overcome with the sadness of the ages. Once I had no fear and was driven by limitless anger. Now I long for a challenge or at least a moment to find purpose.

Each season new groups of humans come and wander among the cages. Marlow guides each one telling story after story of the dangers he faced finding the rare legendary creatures of the past. I was mildly amused with his story of me, considering he described our horrible encounter and how he subdued me with his might. I wonder if the other humans would have been entertained knowing I slept through the entire ordeal. I wonder if their screams would amuse me if I stood and destroyed the cage that holds me with but a shrug.

Thousands upon thousands of human males and females roll by, and I become less and less interested. I would sleep until they destroyed themselves or until the one called Marlow was gone. It would be the blink of an eye in my life, but something keeps me looking at this group of others. Perhaps there is another purpose I have yet to consider.

As a new season starts, we are once again in a huge building called a warehouse. This time I met someone new. A young human girl was hired to sell tickets, and she watches over us at night, feeding the different species and talking to each. I will never forget the first time she came to my prison. She looked at me and smiled. I was familiar with the human smile from Marlow when he collected his money and took advantage of those of us in his sideshow. This one was different. She looked at me, smiled and said, "You don't look very happy to me." She sat in front of my cage and began eating a meal in front of me. I thought about 'happy,' the word that was easy in their English, but I still did not understand the concept well. Happy is a word that perhaps means content, or perhaps satisfied in something but not content. It is a word that has no good meaning for me. I look at her side to side considering 'happy' once again as I have heard it spoken to children and others. "Aren't you happy we came?" I hear often and also, "You will be unhappy when we get home" to the wailing child. Happy seemed to mean so many different things to so many different humans. Perhaps I was only happy when destroying, or perhaps I have and never will be happy. I truly did not know. The human girl was unafraid and visited with me for longer.

I do not truly need to eat as most creatures do. Instead, I have a choice, and sometimes I eat only a few times a year. I do not know why. The great monsters of millions of seasons past ate constantly, while I eat almost never. As this girl sits in front of me, talking to me in her language, I actually feel a little hungry. It is the first time I've felt that way in some time. She was right next to my cage and had little squares that she was crunching on. My hand was as large as she was, and I reached out through the bars to take one of the little squares. She struck my hand.

I did not move back and left my hand there while she waved her finger at me. "That was not polite," she said. I considered the meaning of that word. I had never been polite, but I understood the concept. After all, I could take anything I wanted. She looked at me and asked, "Would you like a cracker?" I nodded in a way meaning affirmative for the human speak.

The girl giggled and put a square in my hand. I put it in my mouth and was amazed at the flavor. I suddenly wanted another. I looked at her and nodded my head up and down again. She gave me another square, and I ate it as well. Each time she would giggle, and each time I was amazed. She had no fear of me. I had never really enjoyed eating; it was just something I did.

"My name is Emma," the girl said. "You're much smarter than Marlow thinks, aren't you? You are not terrifying; I don't think you're scary at all."

The girl was different than the others. She was small and perhaps of only a few years. She told me she was eighteen years old. I understood her language, but I could not speak it as I had never really tried. My vocal cords did not easily resonate as hers did, so it was more difficult for me to mimic their sounds. I could nod "yes" and "no" and acknowledge the child's words. She seemed excited that I could do this, and our interactions became more complex. After a very short time, Marlow was yelling. It was time for her to go.

She gave me quite a few of the crackers, and I enjoyed them. Now I was alone again and waited patiently for nothing in particular.

The next day Emma came back again, and this time she came to me first. She brought me some crackers and set them on a nice circle. I knew this was called a plate. It was a sign of respect that she put this snack on a plate. I sampled each. The flavor was unique, so I ate more. She talked to me about the other animals and began drawing on a pad of something she called paper. For each of the creatures, she created a likeness. I was mesmerized by her skill at recreating the smallest detail as she drew.

Emma then walked to each enclosure and talked to each of the imprisoned creatures. She was patient and kind with each, but she spent most of her time with me, talking about her and her future and how wonderful it was to meet me. I had not heard that in my entire existence. Again, Marlow eventually yelled, and she returned to doing what she did in his service. I saw clearly that she, too, was in her own type of cage, but she wanted to get out.

The next day Emma came to me again and again brought me crackers. This time she put "cheese" on them. I enjoyed the taste even more. It was interesting that a human would show such interest in me. I began noticing things about Emma. Her hair was a different color than everyone else's. It was obvious she had colored it green, and it was equally obvious that not everyone thought it was a good idea. Marlow and some of the others mocked her and did not treat her well because she was different. I knew how she felt. I was perhaps the only one of my kind. I had never met another. It seemed my purpose was simply to exist. I saw things come and go and death took others, but I knew death feared me. Emma walked to each creature again then finally came back to me. She talked to me until Marlow again yelled at her. She frowned, then smiled at me and went back to her tasks.

As the show grew inside the warehouse, more people were

hired. I did not mind, but I noticed how they treated the other creatures trapped in this travesty. As Emma made her rounds to all the animals, it was obvious that the treatment made Emma sad. One day she began talking about releasing us all. I did not care, but it interested me that this human, with only a few years of a race that was an insignificant child compared to myself, cared for us. She asked me what to do as she sat next to my cage while I dutifully ate my crackers. She answered for me and planned what she was going to do. For someone so young, I was impressed with her plan to release us all. I considered how I could relate to her as I could release us all with a shrug, but I did not have the language. I tried to mimic some of the sounds, and she was excited but could not understand me at all.

At night I tried to practice the sounds of the humans and mimic their voices. It was difficult, and the other creatures looked on as some of the sounds I was making began to sound like words. I was trying to let Emma know I could help and actually felt purpose for the first time in untold ages.

Eventually, one evening she came to me, and I listened to her telling me that she would release us today. I thought about it and considered that perhaps it was time to move on. Her plan was simple. She would wait until after the side show was closed and then take all of the creatures to safety. One of the animals, one I knew inspired the human legends of the Chimera, was ill, and Emma wanted to save it. She was sure that once free, the animal would heal and live. I shook my head no to her. She looked over at the animal then back at me. My sight was far more than that of a human or any of the creatures imprisoned with me. To the left of the young animal that she called Liono, I saw the presence of the specter of death watching over and waiting with patience. I was amused at least slightly that the specter of death looked at me cautiously the entire time.

Emma came back later and brought me crackers. She asked me if the animal was better, to which I shook my head no. She went over and spent time with it. She would come back and talk to me, but there was an air of sadness in her that I had not seen in many humans. She honestly cared for those of us locked in this horrible menagerie. I knew she would attempt her plan.

It was later that day that Emma came to see me. I pointed to the animal she had named Liono, and I shook my head again. Death was taking the animal's spirit as I pointed. To me, it was a release, and I was almost thankful that the spirit was free and now happy. To Emma, she saw the animal convulse and fall, then move no more. She cried, and I could see the emotions washing over her. She ran to me, and for the first time, she reached out and put her hand on my massive arms. It had been so long since I had been touched by anything except fear and anger. I did not move and let her cry. Her tears ran down her face, and I felt some strike my hand. Their warmth was chilling, and I could see her in a new light, as more than just a human, as a human with a soul. For so long, I thought I was the only creature with a soul.

Marlow came into the room. "Girl, get away from there. What are you doing?" he yelled. It was then he saw the dead animal lying in the cage. He was furious and began screaming almost uncontrollably. He ran to the cage and opened it. He called for men who came to his aid. They pulled the carcass from the cage and worked to revive it, to no avail. Death had taken the animal, and there was no returning. He screamed over and over and walked to Emma, his face red with anger.

"I should have known not to trust a child," he snarled. Marlow pushed her aside and walked to my prison, he saw the crackers and took them, throwing them at the girl. "It was you who made the animal sick. It was you!"

"I didn't." Emma was still crying and now was scared. "I didn't do anything to Liono! You did! You treat them all horribly!"

Marlow reached back his hand and struck the girl. She fell to the ground grasping her face. He reached out again, and the creatures in the room became agitated. The small dragon screeched, and I smiled as I heard the sounds of the dragons long past. Then my brow furled at the thought of Emma being hit. Flame erupted from the cage that belied the size of the small dragon, and men scattered everywhere. I felt something I had not felt in so long, longer than most would remember. I cared.

The men were swatting at fires everywhere, and the chatter in the room was palpable. Marlow ignored it all. His fury was all-consuming as he picked up Emma and then struck her again. The growl within me grew and grew until I heard my unused vocal cords say a single word that Marlow needed to hear.

"Stop."

The word echoed in the warehouse-like an explosion, and everyone turned towards me. It had been so long since I had uttered a single sound in anger. My voice reverberated in everyone, and the result was fear. Marlow looked at me with disdain thinking the cage held me, but I was not a prisoner of the cage. I was a prisoner of the apathy that had grown within me for thousands of years. This young woman awakened the spirit that allowed me to conquer the world many times over. I waved my hand with but a gesture, and as my fingers touched each of the bars, they shattered easily. The humans built steel in order to cage us all, but I was built of something far stronger, and now I had resolve on my side.

Marlow dropped Emma to the ground. She fell hard, adding to my anger. The other men looked at me and began to panic. They were trapped between me and the fire. I grabbed Marlow. He fit into my hand far too easily. I lifted him above the ground with no effort.

"Put me down, you monster!" he screamed at first with disdain.

He struggled as though he still had some measure of control. I felt his hands try to move mine, and inside I wondered if he felt like the ant trying to lift the mountain in a story Emma had told me. When he realized he could not move me, I saw something in his eyes I had not seen in him before, the sheer terror of the face of fear and impending doom.

I paused then with difficulty and used their words. "I," I began as the realization caught him. "...am not the monster."

I watched him as he realized there was no winning. Perhaps another creature would have had mercy. Perhaps another human would have felt the same. I did not feel anything except for the fury and passion that had driven me for a thousand, thousand lifetimes. I took my other finger and slapped his head. As I threw him across the room, he fell where I could no longer see. Emma lay before me, but men now started throwing ropes and spears at me trying to regain control.

Unbound, I moved through the side show. I saw the other animals cringing in terror inside of their cages. I walked to the first man. I backhanded him in a leisurely move that sent him dozens of feet across the tent. I then ripped the bars from the pixies' cage. Another man used a firearm and shot me over and over. The bullets fell harmlessly from my dense skin, flattened by the impact. I shrugged and ripped away the cage holding the small dragon. As the dragon flew from the cage, it breathed out, and the resulting fire scorched the man to bone in an instant. The charred skeleton crumpled to the ground. Dragon fire was amazingly hot, and I had felt it from full-grown dragons. No creature of normal flesh could survive it.

The misshapen Unicorn was next. I released her with a pinch of my massive hand on her cage, and she stumbled proudly to her freedom. The pride of the unicorns was something I almost admired. Many thousands of years ago, I stumbled upon a group of them, and instead of running, they initially tried to stand their ground with me. As I advanced, they realized there was no winning and rapidly ran, but I would never forget how strong and determined they were in protecting their group.

More men rushed to the area, and now many of the creatures

I freed joined in stopping these men from attacking me. In all my time, no creature had ever fought beside me until today. In all my time, I had always been alone. A new feeling washed over me. What was it about this girl named Emma that opened all of us to something new, a feeling of family, of belonging? Mindlessly, I opened cage after cage as I casually tossed men aside. The pixies tied a man's hair to a wall, and now the unicorn sported a horn covered in blood. It was then that I saw death enter the room.

It would be hard to explain the perceptions of someone who could not see as I did, how swiftly death moved from soul to soul. With but a fraction of a fraction of a second, he took the soul of each man who died and instantly returned for the next. Without their souls, each of the men was gone with no prospect of life in this realm. There were no men left standing. I walked to the warehouse wall and, with contemptuous ease, ripped a gigantic hole into it. I looked at the creatures who had been captive and gestured to the hole now in the wall. Each of them found their way and escaped into the darkness of the night.

As the dragon took flight towards open air, it sang and sprayed fire all over. The warehouse was lit with the crimson gold light of dragon flames lapping the area. As the area burned, I saw a stack of metal in the corner, the bottled fire called propane that men used to try to control the beast it held within. As the canisters started to glow with the dragon's flame, they suddenly exploded, spraying debris everywhere. Pieces of debris bounced harmlessly off me. I wondered how the others would have fared.

I surveyed the open area anew. The devastation was indescribable. Steel, plastic, muslin, and more were shredded and twisted at odd angles. There was a fire still burning from exploded propane tanks and embedded steel speckled in shattered wooden posts from the explosions. An aluminum cage was ripped, and the contents long gone. A similar steel cage was shattered as though the steel bars were made of blown glass. Its contents were gone as well.

The wooden sign lay partially crushed but could easily be

read. The words "Marlow's Side Show Menagerie" were printed in tight lettering with pictures of animals and people around the writing. I reached down and touched the letters on the sign and traced along the edge of one of the pictures. Turning, I saw all the bodies that littered the area. Most would turn away from this type of devastation, but I had to look and see what remained. There in the center, the man, Marlow, was dressed in his tight and handsome tuxedo. His chest was forced into the mud. I could see his face. His head had been twisted completely around. His eyes looked up at me with the blank expression of the dead. He would hurt no one again.

More cages and more bodies were evident in the area. I was used to this type of horror; after all, I had seen horror everywhere I had ever been. There was a movement to my side. I walked to a pile of rubble where a hand stretched out, trying to escape. With contemptuous ease, I moved the rubble and saw the young woman beneath. It was Emma. Her body was battered and bruised, and her face was covered with both blood and dirt. I lifted her as though she were but a feather and cradled her in my arms. She was an innocent victim, collateral damage to what happened here. She was the true hero, the one who would have freed us all.

Emma's breathing was shallow and labored, but her eyes fluttered open. There was recognition in her gaze and a series of other emotions. Understanding, fear, resolve, and something else. I brushed the hair from her face that had been dyed green so that she felt she fit in with the sideshow. She gasped and pulled in a breath. Even in pain, she smiled at me.

"You called him a monster," she said in a raspy voice. "I knew you were smart." She paused again, trying to gain her breath. "Are they free?"

I recognized the raspy voice and the chill hand of death upon her. It would soon close its grip forever. I nodded to her as her eyes showed me one more emotion, relief. Then I used my voice once more, "Yes."

"It was worth it," she struggled with the words as tears ran down her face. "I will go happy knowing the others are free." She struggled, "You will have to find your own crackers now."

I nodded again to her, and the tears continued to stream, creating rivulets of clean skin upon her face. I felt emotions well up in me, and I, too, felt a tear try to come forward, but I was who I was and would not cry. She saw my eyes as she looked at me.

"Don't be sad for me," she said, "I go to a better place, and Marlow will no longer have any of us as his money-making slaves."

Once again, I nodded, and her head shifted slightly. I held her with a tenderness that others would not understand. She coughed, and blood sprayed from her mouth and dripped on her chin. I tried to wipe it away, and she smiled. I watched her gasp and try to pull in air as she looked me in the eye. There was no fear at that moment as she convulsed only slightly.

I saw death enter the room and approach. I knew he was here for her. Death was cautious as he approached, and my suspicions were confirmed. Of all the creatures of this planet, I would go on for all time as death truly feared me. I considered my life and everything I had seen and all the things I had done. Through it all, I was driven by the anger that I had never understood. Perhaps it was the anger of being alone. Perhaps it was the anger of being what I was. I didn't know for sure, even though my wisdom spanned close to the life of this small planet. Death approached and something new wailed inside of me, and in a moment, I opened my mouth and growled, perhaps even screamed. For all that I was, this human child had shown me what I could have been. I would not let her go.

The mists parted, and the specter of death cocked its head to the side. He looked at Emma, and I thought Death smiled. A dark mist rose, and Death retreated. Below me, I heard another cough as Emma fought for her life.

With tender care, I lifted her and carried her to a clear area. I lay her down and reached forward as she coughed and looked up at me. I knew I had to go. As she said, I would miss her crackers. More, I would miss her.

There was no sadness in me, only a purpose. I stood and saw movement again and walked to the movement. Pieces of the Fun House attached to the Sideshow area were crushed and hanging tenuously at off-center angles. A large mirror was before me, and I looked at it with the resolve I have always had. Before me was a reflection. It was a reflection showing arms the size of bridge cables, a chest that could hold the scales of justice, hands that easily destroyed this building and venue, shoulders that could bear the weight of my pain, and a face that had borne far too much. It was a face that struck fear and terror into most, but one young human girl found something more. I spent several minutes looking at that reflection until I heard the voices in the distance. Soon the townsfolk would be there, and soon they would find the devastation. They would not find those that were caged and exploited for so long and instead would only find the bodies of those who exploited them and one young girl who stood above and made a difference. I would be thankful for Emma, as would all who had escaped. Thankful for the future that the others would now have to live. I would be thankful that Emma would now live and hoped that someday she might find us and continue to be the girl she was today.

For me, I had no future and had never had a future. I knew that I would live on. It would be as before Marlow had found me with perhaps something different, thanks to Emma. I took one last look at the reflection in the Funhouse mirror and knew that of all those who were trapped in the little menagerie, only I was a monster. I looked at myself one last time, and I sighed in realization. Jogging away, I disappeared into the night, knowing a monster is not how someone looks but is instead defined by the power of their actions and the trail they leave behind. Perhaps I was not the monster anymore. Perhaps I was something more.

Stung

I have always been very interested in arachnology and, more specifically, in Scorpiology simply because they were so foreign and different from mammals. Most people don't realize there are over two thousand types of scorpions, more or less, but only a few are capable of hurting a human. The forty or so types that could cause major issues give the entire species a bad name. Most scorpions sting about the same as a bee and can actually be a very interesting pet.

Unfortunately, very few of us study scorpions, so we usually end up involved in research about the more dangerous types and rarely get to focus on identifying new species or determining how accurate our research is. It is there that my story starts. It was another typical day in the office, answering a series of emails about useless information or worse, how we were going to make our budget for the next semester. Working at a small college is a nightmare when it comes to budgets simply because you have to have a sponsor or at least someone who will allow funding to go towards entomology and arachnology.

As I toiled with the busy work, there came a knock at the lab door. I had few visitors. I walked to the door, and opened it, expecting another empty hallway. The students were sometimes immature, and pranks happened. Instead, a man in uniform stood before me with a series of papers in his hand. His designation noted him as a Sherriff, and his crisp tan uniform was filled by a mountain of a man.

"Professor Aziz?" he asked.

"Yes," I replied, "I am Matthew Aziz. How can I help you?"

"Well," the Sherriff began, "My Name is Caruthers. I am from Isabel, a little town about twenty miles from here. We have a bit of a mystery, and you are pretty much the last hope I have of identifying a poison and a mark on a body."

"I don't know that I've ever been anyone's last hope," I said.

"I don't know that I've ever seen anything like this before, so I think we're kind of in the same boat," Sherriff Caruthers said. "I have three deaths on my hands, and no weapon, no suspects, and not even the FBI can tell me anything about how it was done."

"So why reach out to me?" I asked.

"Well, at least that's easy," the sheriff said. "You had a student here named Johnson. He apparently was in your class a few years ago and is now working for our office. When he saw the mark, he said it looked like a scorpion sting you showed them years ago, but it was bigger. On a whim and a prayer, I decided to come here."

"Larry Johnson?" I asked. "He was a great student, and I'm glad he was paying attention, but it's unlikely a scorpion killed someone. Most of them won't hurt you, and it'll be more like a bee sting."

"Didn't I just say this was a whim and a prayer move?" the sheriff replied. "If I had anywhere else to go, I would not be on this bug hunt talking to you in the middle of nowhere about something I know damn well shouldn't be possible. You would have expected those morons at the FBI to come up with something, but they shook their head and moved on faster than a Kansas tornado."

I laughed at the comparison but thought about it and decided, what the heck. "Let's see what you got, and I hope I can be of some help," I said.

The sheriff sat down a large envelope on the table in front of me. He opened it and slid out a series of about forty pictures. All of them were eight and a half by eleven and all of them were of different angles to a body. The pictures on top of the pile were at a location, but the bulk of the pictures had been taken at the morgue during an autopsy. They included a series of pictures that were close up of what could only be described as a hole in the body's back. I started paying more attention as the photos became more focused on that hole. As the pictures got closer and closer, I saw that Johnson may have been paying more attention than I was. If you didn't know the scale in the extreme closeup, you would have automatically said scorpion sting, but the scale was off. As I looked closer, I realized the if a scorpion did this, it would have to be several hundred times larger than any scorpion on file.

"We need to give Johnson an 'A'," I said. "If I hadn't looked at any other pictures except the last two, I would have told you it was a scorpion in an instant. But knowing the scale, and just some rough measurements, this scorpion may well have walked outside and flipped a car over after it was done with this person. I'm betting you're looking for a copycat or someone that made a scorpion cane or weapon."

"That's what Johnson had to say, he said the idea of this was fascinating, but it wasn't valid." Caruthers noted. "But when he looked at the toxicology he was baffled. He said it was an exact match to a scorpion, as well. He started babbling about mutations and then went back to copycats. Then he suggested I come to see you."

I laughed for a moment. "I bet he was driving you nuts. He made a lab partner crazy with the 'fascinating' talk. Honestly, I think he watched too many episodes of Star Trek when he was young and thought he was Spock." I looked over the toxicology report and continued reading. Along with the toxicology report was a mass spectrometer report on portions of the poison and DNA. I shook my head as I walked over to the bookcase on my wall. I pulled out a well-worn book and flipped through some pages, as I sat down. "Your report has this for an exact match to Androctonus Australis, but these numbers don't make sense. A normal scorpion sting is about half a milliliter. Some of the more exotic venoms sell for as much as $5,000 a gram on the black market. Your report here says the wound had 170 grams of venom in it. That means it would have cost about $800,000 and been about as much as a mid-size energy drink. Killing someone with this would not only be overkill, but it would also be a waste of money. It would have taken a year to milk scorpions to get that much. Are you sure this report is right?"

"Yeah, the lab geek we have wanted to know if we could sell it afterwards, and your guy Johnson wanted to have it donated to your school," the Sherriff stated. "There is a vial of this stuff, and they guessed there could have been more spilled out on the sides at the scene, that could not be collected. The whole thing is pretty much geek talk to me."

"I get it sheriff," I said. "This is one of the weirder things you could have brought to me, and I'm sitting here trying to think of anyone in the world where you could get this much venom in one spot. I know some exotic collectors that have a few grams, maybe, and there is an institute in London that might have a few more. This would have been a huge ordeal, and I'm not sure how anybody could pull it together. The British Museum of Natural History would be the best starting point as they publish quite a bit about different scorpions. But they would probably go crazy knowing there was this much venom anywhere. Who in the world was killed by this? Did they work with scorpions? Tell me, were they somebody special? Honestly, they must have died in seconds. With this much venom, it's a lot like using an atomic bomb to hunt mosquitoes. The venom affects the central nervous system. This person must have locked up within seconds then probably broke their own spine from the convulsions. It's not a very pleasant way to go. I still don't get it. Why use scorpion venom? Was your killer trying to say something? Was there some type of gang or another group making a statement?"

"Those are all pretty good questions," the sheriff stated. "I'm looking for motive, but there doesn't seem to be any." He pulled out a small pad and then started flipping through it. "The man is a nobody. Thirty-two years old without any real family or friends. Had a lot of online connections but nothing that was of any consequence. Played a ton of video games and was a video game designer. Had a huge collection of "Dungeons and Dragons" paraphernalia, but nothing that had anything to do with scorpions. No animals and not much of anything else. This is some geek that went down to the corner bar twice a week and had a cheeseburger and a beer and spent the rest of his time talking to other geeks about video games. The only thing we found from looking around was one person in a chat room who said this guy had a new girlfriend. We didn't find a girlfriend or even any evidence this guy knew what to do with a girl."

"That seems pretty harsh," I said. "I wonder if you would say the same about me?"

"Yeah, you're pretty much the same," Caruthers chuckled as he pulled out a picture of a normal-looking white man. "I ran background on you, and it reads pretty much like this guy. Except you spend all your time playing with scorpions, and he spent all his time playing on the Internet. You do have an advantage that you were married once. Looks like she's off in California with some other guy while you sit here and teach people about little bugs."

"Ouch," I laughed. "That was pretty harsh."

The Sheriff shrugged his shoulders and straightened his uniform a little. He was a really big guy. He reminded me of the sheriff from the movie 'Lake Placid.' I looked him over again and wondered if he had a wife and kids, and a cute little picket fence with a dog in the backyard.

"I'm not sure what I can do for you past what I've told you," I said. "Maybe I should just sit around and play with my scorpions."

"Don't get all hurt," the Sherriff said. "You didn't expect me to come down here not knowing anything about you?"

"Actually, it would be more accurate to say I didn't expect you to come down here."

The Sheriff's phone rang, and he took out an old flip phone and walked over to the door. I could hear him talking, and someone on the other side of the phone must have been relatively frantic. Sheriff Caruthers began looking irritated almost immediately. He hung up the phone and came over to me.

"Would you like to take a ride with me?" he asked.

"Why in the world would I want to take a ride with you?" I asked, perhaps still a little irritated at his opinion of me.

"Because there's been another killing, and Johnson is pretty sure that it's the same thing," the Sherriff replied.

In spite of my somewhat petty feelings at the moment, I was also fascinated by the idea of using scorpion venom as a weapon, so I said the only thing that came to my mind, "Why not."

I closed up the lab, and the two of us left as I locked the door. I laughed to myself because there wasn't much reason to lock the door, given that only geeks like me would be interested in much inside the lab. Still, I did have a supply of scorpion venom, and apparently, that was in high demand right now. I didn't want to contribute to the open market without making money for the school.

The sheriff's car was the standard Crown Victoria monster that most officers drive and had numerous decals on the brown and gold finish. I often wondered why sheriff's officers were pegged with boring colors like tan and brown, and police officers got all sorts of snazzy colors. It was rare to see anything besides dull mud brown in a sheriff's repertoire.

"Why do they always make sheriff's cars brown?" I asked as we pulled out of the parking lot.

"That's easy," the sheriff stated. "We're usually the ones digging everyone else out of the crap, and it doesn't show up on our uniform as bad."

"Our sheriff has a blue car," I said.

"Your sheriff has an easy job," Caruthers said. "I hear crime is down to almost nothing in your little town."

"Seems like the criminals don't like it here anymore," I said. "At least that's what he says. They've all just seemed to disappear."

67

"I wish he would share that trick with me," Caruthers replied. "It would be nice for crime to disappear."

I laughed and then was quiet as we drove out the edge of our small town.

"I never did ask you where you're from," I said. "Actually, I didn't ask to see your credentials either. Kinda got caught up in somebody hanging around with $800,000 worth of scorpion venom. You're not trying to kidnap me, are you?"

The sheriff glanced at me with obvious disdain. "No."

"So, how far are we going?" I asked as he got on the Expressway at the edge of town.

"About that far," he replied as we were speeding along. He had the lights flashing but no siren. It was not so busy that he needed it, and as we approached cars, he would turn it on for a moment until he was past them and then turn it off. Five minutes later, we got off at a small exit that just had a number on it. We turned right, and a few hundred yards ahead, I saw several vehicles with flashing lights. The car pulled over, and the big man behind the wheel pushed his way out of the car. I stepped out as well.

I recognized Johnson as he walked over to us and held out his hand to me. "Howdy Professor."

"Howdy," I said. "Was nice to see you remembered something I taught."

"I'm not so sure I want to right now sir," Johnson replied, pointing to the clearing ahead. "This one will blow your mind."

I wasn't sure what to expect but followed Johnson with the sheriff in tow until we came to a small clearing. Men were walking around taking pictures, and several were pouring casts onto the ground. In the center of it all was a body. It was a man of about twenty-five. His eyes were cloudy as he stared up into a sky he would never see again. His face was slightly discolored, and there was a tear on the front of his bright red t-shirt. Johnson knelt down and put a pair of gloves on. He lifted the shirt and showed me a wound about an inch across. "The medical examiner isn't here yet. I bet this mark matches the one on the other body. Walk over here. This time there was more." Johnson covered the wound with the shirt again and walked around the site. "Look over here."

As we walked around where several men were doing castings, we saw the indentations in the ground. They were spread wide, about eight feet across between two indentations. I knelt for a moment and looked at the indentations and saw something familiar. I walked to the other side of one of the indentations and knelt. I looked at it without touching it.

"This is pretty ridiculous but accurate. The end indentations are correct, but if this is right, these distances would mean that the scorpion in question would be approximately sixteen feet long. The largest scorpion to ever walk the earth was only about three feet long. It's ridiculous to assume that a scorpion could get this big. The stress factors alone on the exoskeleton would be difficult, if not impossible, to calculate. This is cute for a movie, but in reality, it just doesn't make any sense."

"I already said that to them, and they had to find you," came a female voice from behind. "Your ex-student and the sheriff didn't want to listen to me."

I turned and saw a young woman of about thirty, her long red hair went about halfway down her back and was pulled into a tight ponytail. Her eyes were dark brown, making me wonder if her hair coloring was natural. Usually, redheads had green eyes. The woman was dressed in a tight pantsuit with an equally tight jacket, and I could see the outline of a weapon under her arm.

"They will have to listen if they want me as an expert," I said.

"I am well aware of your expertise," the woman said. "My

name is Elizabeth, Elizabeth Seal.”

“Didn't I read a paper from you about spider and scorpion interactions in the wild?” I asked.

“It's nice to know that somebody read it,” Elizabeth said. “I think I only had four peers agree with me. Most of them think that scorpions and spiders look for each other. I can almost conclusively prove that they stay away from each other. I'm sorry you had to come all the way out here. The measurements and, of course, the amount of venom used is ridiculous. There is no way that there would be a scorpion big enough to make these tracks. This has to be some type of stunt by someone who has access to either a lot of scorpions or a lot of money. What we need to do is look at the victims and determine a motive for killing them.”

Sheriff Carruthers spoke up, “Miss Seal is here with the FBI advising us on how we should approach this case. Her expertise is with unique cases. I pretty much equate her to that television show with the two FBI agents who chase nut cases.”

“I'm sure you mean the X Files,” I said. “I really like that show. I didn't think there really was an FBI section that did stuff like that.”

“It's not really a section,” Elizabeth said. “It's more like just me. I keep getting thrown the strange sideways cases. It would really be nice if someone actually respected my expertise instead of just tossing me to the side.”

“Well guys, I hate to say it, but Miss Seal is correct. You should be looking at the people because there is no scorpion this large. If there was, we would have found it a long time ago. Actually, if there was, it probably would have killed all of us off by now rather than picking particular people. It's more likely that there is a better explanation. As far as the venom, I'd like a sample to see if it is somehow being synthesized. That's kind of the strange thing. No one will spend $1,000,000 just to kill somebody.”

Johnson looked at the sheriff, and the sheriff nodded to him.

Johnson went to the car and brought back a small vial. "I had this pulled in case you asked," Johnson said.

"Well, the only question now is how do I get back to my lab?" I stated.

"I'll take you," Elizabeth said. "I can't do much here anymore, and we can talk along the way. I can also help you do the analysis if you are okay with that."

I was impressed with the professionalism of this young woman, and I quickly agreed. In a matter of moments, we were on the road, and Elizabeth proved to be quite an interesting person. We talked in-depth about the case and how scorpions were being targeted. We both agreed that there was no easy way for a scorpion to be anywhere near that large. Then we started talking about why someone would go to create such elaborate measures. Then the discussion came around to how to execute that coup de grace without anyone seeing and with what type of weapon. We discussed the unique entry point and how elegant the weapon must be to inject venom and create such a convincing scorpion mark.

"I thought at first it was your student, Johnson." Elizabeth said. "He was so excited about the prospect and beaming with the idea that it could be a giant scorpion."

"He always was a little bit overzealous," I said.

"For a moment, I thought it was the right answer, and there was a giant scorpion, but it just didn't make sense that there were no tracks at the first murder," Elizabeth continued.

"Would there have been tracks?" I asked.

"Of course, there would have been tracks," Elizabeth said, "given the creature's size, it would have weighed enough for the pins at the feet to pierce just about anything. I mean, think of the equation of how many pounds per square inch would be applied on those legs."

"The way I figure it, the amount would be almost one ton per square inch," I said.

"I was guessing a little more than that," Elizabeth said. "If we can figure out where this venom came from, it will put us on the way to catching the killer."

"How would you suggest we go about doing that?" I laughed. "Venom is hard to come by, and this much, well, if it was manufactured, there aren't many places that could do it."

"I agree with you," Elizabeth replied, "But I know that your lab could do it, and there are about fifty others around the country in various institutions."

"It would be tedious, and the process would be more expensive than the payoff," I said.

"But if you could do it, then how would you go about it?" Elizabeth asked. "Maybe that will give us a clue."

I knew she was serious as I looked into her eyes. I knew she would never let go of this idea, so I had no choice but to go along with it for the moment. "Well, I suppose I would start with deciding what type of venom to make."

"We already know that," she replied. "So, once you had the venom, what would you do next."

"Well, the proper way to go about it and the only way I know of would be to grow the venom glands through genetic splicing. I would have to take eggs from the scorpions, which, as you know, are pretty easy to get, and then splice them so that they were just growing the venom glands. It's been done with snakes, but an arachnid would be a little harder." I paced for a moment. "There's no way that we could get over the amount of venom that was produced in this particular case. We're back to some type of monster that made the footprints."

"We both know that isn't possible," Elizabeth replied.

"What if it was?" I asked.

"It's a ridiculous option to even consider," she replied. "How could you even breed something like that?"

"Perhaps it's not so ridiculous," I said. "Maybe we just need to look at it from a different point of view. If you think about it, the amount of venom we found would be impossible to get from thousands of small venom glands. It's one of the reasons that the venom is so expensive. What if a creature was made and spliced with larger creatures or even had its DNA altered so it would be this large? Whoever made it wasn't expecting it to be able to move; they just wanted the venom. A creature that size would be able to create enough venom to make someone very rich very fast."

"That's simply ridiculous," Elizabeth said. "Anyone that would even try something like that would have to be psychotic."

"Or need the money really bad," I replied.

"Okay," she said, "let's dump this idea and go get something to eat for a moment. I have a headache now."

"Sure," I said. "My car is in the garage, and we can take it over to the diner."

"I can drive," Elizabeth said.

"I don't get to have guests for dinner often," I said. "I would rather treat you."

Elizabeth nodded in consent, and I motioned towards the door. I opened the door from the lab, and we went down the small hallway toward the garage.

"It is a cool idea," I said. "Wouldn't it be amazing to see something like that?"

"It would be more amazing to kill it and whoever made it," Elizabeth said.

"Yeah," I said. "Maybe you're right."

I opened the door to the garage. The dim lights showed very little. The garage was very large one hundred cars could be parked in it easily. It was left over from when the college had a large auto shop class. Somehow, I got access to it and kept it for my pet projects. In the corner near the door, my car waited for us. The 1964 Corvette was a classic and had been my dream car for a long time. It took a lot of work for me to get it, but I was so happy with the way it drove.

"Aren't there any lights in here?" Elizabeth said.

"I need to fix some of them," I replied. "They have been broken for a little while. Can you see my car?"

"Yes, I can," Elizabeth said. "I'll help you fix those lights when we get back if you want, and we can talk about who could have done this."

I walked around the side of the car door with Elizabeth and was about to open her door and then stopped. I looked at her and smiled. "It was such a good paper that you wrote."

"Okay, um, thanks," she replied.

"I know who did this, and it was an accident," I said.

"Who?" Elizabeth asked.

I knocked on the side of the door twice. There was a huge scratching behind Elizabeth. She turned just as the claw grabbed her. I was amazed at the speed that this creature had developed. I watched Elizabeth gasp and look first to me and then the creature holding her.

"How, why?" she sputtered.

"It was for the money, of course," I said. "My program was about to be cancelled, and the school was just about to be closed. This one magnificent creature will save us all and already has. Usually, he cleans up after himself by eating his kills, but this last time, well, these last two times, he was interrupted. I know it seems horrible, but we've been eliminating the people in our way while we make money with the venom. I was amazed at how intelligent this animal was and how easy it was to train him when he was little. Now he's docile with me and pretty much will eat anything I point out. I'll make sure your superiors know that you left. I'm sorry there won't be any trace."

Elizabeth struggled with the claw and reached for her weapon. She tried to pull it out, but her arms were pinned tight, and she couldn't get any leverage. As she tried to get it and aim at the gigantic scorpion, I knocked on the car door three times, and the claw closed tight.

It only took a moment, and then Elizabeth was pressed into the maw of the scorpion, never to be seen again.

I smiled for a moment and reached up and patted the claw of this creature I had raised from an egg. I turned and walked back to the door and to my office. When I got there, the phone was ringing. I answered.

"Hello," I said.

"This is sheriff Caruthers," he said. "Is that FBI lady still there?"

"No Sir," I said. "I think her car is still here, but she left a little while ago with another agent. Something about an alien."

"Just like the FBI to leave us like that," he replied. "Did you two come up with anything?" he asked.

"Pretty much the same as when we left you," I said. "This has to be some kind of hoax. Elizabeth agreed, and I guess that's why she left. Do you want me to call anyone else?"

"That won't be necessary," the Sherriff sighed. "We will look around our county and see what we can find. If you come up with anything, you let me know."

"I'll do that," I replied. "If you see Elizabeth, tell her I'd like to see her for dinner sometime."

The sheriff laughed, "Sure I will."

The phone went dead, and I sat there for a moment. The few people in the shop class would take apart the Crown Victoria and sell it for parts. Anything with serial numbers would be dumped or melted down. We'll make sure that our town and our school are around for a long time. My little pet, well, he'll be hungry again soon, and there's always someone causing trouble.

Small Solace

The knocking door was incessant but not overly loud. It thrummed like a slow, methodical machine or a beating drum from a forgotten Amazon tribe. When Tilly answered the door, she was greeted by a tall man with a black suit, black oxfords, a crisp black shirt and tie, and a small black leather padfolio.

"Sorry to disturb you, ma'am," the man said. "Allow me to introduce myself." The man handed Tilly a card that simply said, "Grimace Growler" with the tagline, "Lesser of the Evils." "My name is Grimace. I'm here to collect on your debt."

"But I have no debts," Tilly said. "I have no debts at all."

"We don't make mistakes," Grimace said. "I am here to collect on your soul. If I cannot collect your soul, the greater of two evils will take your child's soul as well. We always get what we want."

"I never made a deal for my soul," Tilly shivered. "I wouldn't give up my soul."

"Nevertheless, you did exactly that." Grimace pulled out a single piece of parchment. "Did you not, on May 2nd of this year, while standing over your father, plead that you would do anything to ensure that he lived."

"I did," Tilly replied. "But I made no bargain at the time."

"Your father is still living?" Grimace asked.

"He did live," Tilly replied.

"The delivery of your needs constitutes a binding contract, and as such, we are entitled to your soul."

Tilly sighed; she remembered her father gasping for breath.

COVID almost took him away. She would have given anything not to lose her father.

"What do I have to do?" Tilly said.

"It's pretty easy," said Grimace. "All you have to do is sign these papers, and we will execute later." Grimace brought out a huge stack of papers and handed them to her. On the last page was a small flag and a spot for her to sign. "I'm glad you chose the lesser, as I would hate for you to experience the greater of two evils."

Tilly took her time and began reading over the contract. "I will want to take a moment and read this."

"Of course, of course," Grimace said.

It took time, and finally, Tilly stood. "It says here on page 467 that I am entitled to proof that the actual event was of your doing. I would like to see that proof immediately."

"I will have to get back to you; I was not given that proof," Grimace said.

"Then, according to page 488, this contract is null and void as all proof must be presented with the contract," Tilly smiled.

Grimace took the contract from her and put it back in his padfolio. Tilly wasn't sure how to read his smile as a smile of victory or defeat, but he did smile as he tipped his hat and said, "Well played, good day." Then he walked out of the door and was gone.

Beatrice

I walked through the beautiful house once more. It would be hard letting go of all the memories. The spiral staircase that wound its way up to the second floor boasted dozens of pictures of our family. The deep mahogany wood used for the railings, the staircase, and the ornate walls gave the room an eerie red glow when the sunlight shone through the windows at the top of the staircase. No matter what the time of day, it just felt warm and perhaps a little foreboding.

I started walking up the staircase to look at the pictures. At the bottom of the stairs was one of my great, great grandfathers, from World War I. He looked crisp in his uniform and had the stoic expression of many in those days. Another step and there was another picture of him and his wife, my great, great grandmother. There were aunts and uncles and dozens of others. Some I knew and some I did not. I spent time looking at the pictures, slightly melancholy for the moment, considering what other options there may be to save our home.

Our family had been prominent in the area for some time. Much of the local infrastructure was developed by my great grandparents, and my great, great, great grandmother stood over them all. She built this house and put her life's blood into it. It was often said that she watched over us all and kept the town, Felicity, safe. She swore that one of us would live in this house for all time, and we would continue to protect our interests and the interests of Felicity. That promise would be broken as the town had faded away with the factories first and then the people. Everything was to be packed and sent to a new home a hundred miles away in the middle of nowhere. This site would soon be leveled along with the rest of the town. An amusement park was being built here, and the entire town would soon be gone.

My father and I would soon profit from the sale of the land, but there was little else to do. We tried everything and were down to our last pennies trying to save the house and our city. Many of the townspeople wanted to hold on, but they were just out of money.

Joe, the local grocer, was down to a few customers a week. He could barely pay his electric bill. A few older families hung on, living off their retirement, but most were gone, their houses boarded up like our lives had been. There were no more factories, no more workers, and little else.

At the local diner, Sarah worker herself to the bone with no help. Dad and I would visit each morning for breakfast, and occasionally people would stop in. We all talked about the good days and wished the interstate had not ripped the last hope of success from us.

Of the thousand-plus people and two hundred homes, now there were maybe fifty remaining. I was saddened by it all. I believed in our family.

This location was perfectly placed for what was intended. I'm not sure why anyone cared. I made my way to the top of the stairs and stared at the picture of Beatrice, the founder of all of Felicity, the builder of this house. I got a tear in my eye. She would be saddened by this move and would have said what she always said to people, "We will find a way."

I looked at the picture and remembered my grandfather telling me stories of her tenacity. Beatrice would fight for everything. She had once run off the bad element from the city and did not stop there. She would have found a way; she was the core of what we needed.

I had tried the Internet for help. Kickstarter, GoFundMe, and more, but who had heard of Felicity? It was just another small city that was dying and would soon be gone. I stared at Beatrice and wished with all my heart she was here to help. The glint of her eyes in the portrait was amazing. She almost looked alive as I closed my eyes and wiped away a tear.

I turned and walked down the stairs. I'd walked down four stairs and I heard the bulldozers outside. The workers were unloading heavy equipment and starting to set up. I wondered if the papers had been signed. I thought about how deeply this would hurt my father. First, he lost my mom, and now this.

I heard a light whine behind me. I looked around and saw nothing. The whine became a shrill cry and then a scream. I finally saw the picture of Beatrice change. The once pristine photo was now contorted in rage. Not knowing what to do, I ran down the stairs and out the door as the scream became louder and louder. It seemed to echo not only in the air but inside my mind. As I ran a little further, I saw the ground around the house fall away. Outside, I could see people holding their ears. The shrill cry of doom was upon us. It was like some lost and wicked sound, like the banshee of ancient lore.

The ground seemed alive and shivered as if in terror. Then, a mere matter of minutes later, a perfect circle surrounded the house twenty feet deep. The contractors in the area came over and looked down into the hole as silence once again was restored.

The house was now surrounded by an enormous sinkhole. There was no way to get in safely; no equipment could get through it.

The amusement company decided the chances of another sinkhole were too great. They backed out of the contract. Now the home stands, still watching over what's left of the small city.

What I thought would be bad for us turned out to be a major boon. Felicity is now a tourist center. The city is booming with the story of Beatrice. Paranormal researchers come from far and wide to see this phenomenon and walk the bridge we constructed to the house. Sarah has five staff now to keep up with making food. Real estate has jumped, and houses are no longer empty. Joe can't keep his shelves stocked. Many of the remaining townspeople have opened small shops with trinkets and books about the paranormal. People line up to come to the house, talk to Dad and me, and of course, see the picture.

I have told my story a hundred times, and it never gets old. The disbelievers be damned. When they go into the house, they see Beatrice on the top of the staircase smiling down as if she had found a way to save us all. My father and I are living in our house again. The rooms creak at night, and we are safe and happy knowing our family is safe. Beatrice, well, she makes herself known, and occasionally in the morning, we hear the shrill scream, and the news crews show up again.

Countdown

The lights came on in the room as President Mitchel walked to his opulent desk. Startled, he saw a figure sitting in the shadows. It stood and moved towards him.

"How did you get in here?" the president asked. "I am…"

The President's words were cut short when he saw the Glock-17 pointed at him. "Please sit down."

"Okay," the President replied, "You know you can't get out of here alive. There are guards everywhere. I can call out, and you will be killed instantly."

"Not quite instantly. You would be dead long before they got a shot at me. It's late. Remember? You told them you would be busy for a while. You said you needed time to think. We will have some time together. Sit down, let's talk."

"Who are you?" The President sat down.

"You could find me in your systems if you knew how. At least maybe your people could; they can be quite resourceful. I doubt you have ever done much in your life but lead others. I believe your bio said you worked as a barista at one time, but I could not confirm that. True leaders work with their team, not just above them. True leaders know how to do every job that reports to them. After all, how can a leader lead if he doesn't know where he is going? No matter, no fortune cookie stuff today. I have had a strange week thanks to you, and this will be the end of it. You can call me Michael."

"Well, Michael, what is it that you want?" The President asked. "You have my attention at least."

"Justice, I suppose. I was hired by a series of men who believe in justice. They told me a story about that clock you have over there, the countdown timer with the unique symbols on it."

"What about it?" the President asked, his voice with a little quaver.

"They told me a story about aliens, and our environment, a series of human beings eliminated, to be taken by electronic means. It was a story about a President wanting to rid the world of opposition. A story about a group of people putting themselves above the rest. They explained to me that a lot of the last few years have been about trying to control people. They showed me how media was being used in the United States, Russia, and China to force preparation for a lot of missing people. They explained that the people would barely be missed with the preparation being put in place. These people, who believe in justice, they tried to go through normal measures to bring out the truth. Unfortunately, it would not work as the alien forces were helping the governments destabilize the masses and control the flow of information."

"Sounds a bit crazy," the President was sweating but in control again. "What does that have to do with me?"

"Well, according to these men, you brokered a deal with the aliens to quietly take people from the planet. They would be transported for slavery, breeding stock, and food. It all seemed a little medieval until I confirmed it. I was impressed with the technology. The synchronous targeting of such a large number of people was impressive. All these people would disappear at the appointed time, never to be seen again. Beam me up, Scotty."

"Confirmed it? How could you do that?" The quaver was back. "Seems to me you need help, Mister, I mean Michael. I can find you some help if you like."

"No, thank you. I am quite sane and always in control. It helps me in my line of work. I am an assassin. I am very good at my job. I was for you, this country, and many people who needed assistance with justice. I am not so deluded to think I am a role model or a hero. I just don't suffer from the pain that other men do in eliminating targets. This makes me particularly effective as an assassin. Anyway, my specialty is finding high profile and hidden targets. The men who hired me gave me more than enough to track down the Crycksthis even though they are quite elusive. They were hidden in plain sight, making it almost an easy task. They were direct in their communications with me. It is an interesting race. I believe they would have been happy to talk to me for longer. They had not encountered anyone like me. They were impressed with my tenacity and ability. When I eliminated all of your guards, yes, all ten of them, the Crycksthis were quite taken by the speed and accuracy of my technique. They offered me a position, but I politely turned it down. We spent the afternoon speaking about this world, you, and the myriad of people they have encountered. We reviewed the current contract, and it was obvious these aliens were very good businessmen, but they did not like some of the things I pointed out to them. In our review, we determined your negotiations gave them the ability to return. They also explained you were having issues picking targets, and they were growing weary of the delays and debates. Your country's representatives had met several times to clear things up, but no one could agree on terms. The Crycksthis did not feel this was profitable for them and were ready to withdraw. I have to say I was impressed with one part. The goal was in the right place, removal of complex carbon molecules, including plastics and PFAS. This would undo a lot of the damage done in the last negotiation when they gave you the formula for plastic. That too was a surprise."

"I'm glad you approve." the President was watching the doors and looking for a way to escape.

"If you run, I will just shoot you," Michael said. "I like how the clock only has three minutes remaining. How did you get them to all agree on targets?"

"I suppose there is no point denying what you already know," the President replied. "I convinced everyone to pick their political opponents and a portion of the poor worldwide."

"It was a good plan for you," Michael said. "We discussed the matter transmitters and how they worked. It took very little time for me to understand that the extraction would be over in seconds and one million people would just disappear, instantly transporting to their stasis ships. A million people gone in an instant. You picked one million targets for twenty years of seclusion. I was a little more aggressive. I picked a little over ten million targets in exchange for 500 years. The Crycksthis not only agreed, but they also gave me a bonus. For ten million, they would not return. Apparently, we are a little too warlike and harder to sell. The fact that their technology was clearly advanced, but their weapons were inferior to ours, was disturbing to them. They would have been afraid of me even with their matter transmitters if I had not explained trust and justice to them first."

"You made a deal?" the President asked with a nervous voice. "What deal?" The President looked to his desk.

"No worries now, all the Crycksthis phones have been removed except mine. I also have this watch. Not only does it mimic your countdown clock, but it removed any possibility of me being targeted by the matter transmitters. The look on your face tells me you didn't know this even existed," Michael noted. "Look, thirty seconds left."

"What did you do?" The President stood slightly with obvious discomfort.

"I made a great deal. Sure, we will have a few years of problems, but they will work out pretty quickly. There are a little over seven million active politicians in the world, and soon we will start at ground zero. There are also about three million excessive supporters of politicians that will go too. The far left, the far right, the radical wings of the world. You know, the ones who don't support people, rich or poor? Anyway, enjoy your trip."

The clock counted down to zero. The President disappeared in a blinding blue-white flash. Michael holstered his weapon, turned off the lights, and left the room. Tomorrow would be chaos, but it was better than what could have been. The world had a chance, and the people that mattered would be able to rebuild. Michael would now know that justice had been served.

Apprehension

I know it is coming. There can be no doubt. The time is right, and like clockwork, he will be here soon. I'm struggling today. I have done my chores, and I have made sure all of his idiosyncrasies are addressed. It has not been easy because I, too, want to have a life. I have goals. I have desires, passions, and I want to do more than just serve a brutal master.

I have done all I could with the children. They, too, are in patient wait for him. Whether it is going to be a good night or a bad night will be decided in the first few minutes of his arrival. I dread the sound of his key in the lock because I know that in just a few minutes, my evening will be decided. There will be either a good or bad night no matter what I did. Far worse, my daughter will suffer with me, and my son will be transformed further and further into the monster that I now serve.

I wouldn't give up my children for anything, but I had hoped for a better life. I had hoped to be able to make a difference in the lives of others. I had hoped to make a difference in my own life and raise my children to always do what is right. Instead, we are but ping pong balls in an ocean storm, thrown by the wind without regard to our individuality. I fear my son will one day be the storm.

I look at my daughter as she peers at the door and notice a tear in her eye. The anticipation is the hardest part. I check my dress and make sure it is buttoned up, and I am the picture of a conservative woman. I make sure that my makeup is not overdone and looks as though I wear none. I wring my hands tight around the still damp dishtowel and realize that my knuckles are white from the strain.

I feel as though I can feel the second hand click from *tick* to *tock* finding myself assailed by the sounds of phantom echoes. If only my feelings were unwarranted. If only this nightmare could be overcome. For such a long time, I knew it was my fault. If I would just wait it would get better. If I would just wait. My family knows that he is such a good person, taking care of his family. But no one seems to see the reality of my world. No one can know except those of us who live it. I tried to get help and instead was told I was imagining things. They asked if I wanted a prescription.

I hear the click of the key, and the door swings open. My heart breaks at the start of another night. I can only hope to be a shield to my children for one more night. The sound is deafening as I hear the words repeated all too often, "Honey, I'm home."

I panic. Am I doing the right thing? I straighten and walk to him. I have prepared for so long. Will it finally be over?

"Where are the kids," he asks.

"They are in their rooms," I reply, knowing he will not check on them. They are just a means of control over me. They were conceived so I could not leave him; I could only fall deeper into his trap.

"Is my dinner ready?" he asked, looking at me. "You look nice tonight."

I looked down at myself. Dressed in thrift store bargains that I scraped to acquire. I made sure they were humble so no one would notice me, and I would be his slave. At least it was not for all time.

"Yes," I said, "Your dinner is in the kitchen."

"The kitchen," he eyes me suspiciously. "We rarely eat in the kitchen. Is this a special day, or did you fall behind again? Do we need to get the whip?"

I cringed, knowing I would be beaten severely if I did not think fast. "No, I just thought it would be easier, and I could clean up, afterward to keep the kitchen perfect. With the children asleep, it will be quieter as well."

"Quiet?" he asked me. "I can be as noisy as I want. This is my house. It is my money, my children; all of this is mine. I can do as I see fit." His voice rose as he spoke.

"I know you can," I replied and lowered my head. He knew he had won again. Any time I felt strong or reached out, he tightened the noose. He made sure I could not think, react, or get help. People who met him thought he was so charming, but in reality, he was a monster. Even monsters can be beaten.

We walked into the kitchen. On the table was an envelope and a file folder.

"What's this," he asked.

"Let me get your dinner," I said, "You can read while I serve you."

"Serve me," his grin was wicked and aloof. He knew he was in control. He picked up the papers first and looked at the folder. His face changed from control to anger. "Where did you get these? This is from my private files." His eyes were full of fury. "You are going to pay for this intrusion into my privacy." He started to stand.

"Read the envelope first," I said. "Then do as you may."

His eyes never left me, but he sat back down in the simple oak chair and picked up the envelope.

I watched him read the letter. His eyes widened. I knew the words by heart.

Husband,

I found your files when I was cleaning. You left them out, and I saw the significance immediately. Since I have my degree in accounting, it was easy for me to reverse engineer the numbers and determine that you have stolen over twenty million dollars from your partners. The technique was subtle, but if you remember, I was always better than you at accounting. If you had not forced me into your life and stolen my future, I would have found success as well. Now we will see if I can succeed and do it the right way.

These files were shared with your partners last week, and they wanted me to set up dinner this way tonight. I was apprehensive but they assured me I was safe now. I had a hard time believing it.

Don't worry. The kids and I will be fine. Without my asking, I was given a generous stake to start a new life. It is not much, but it is enough to live a few years easily without a job or indefinitely, if I achieve my success.

Thank you for giving me two wonderful children, but this is goodbye,

His eyes were intense, "Do you think you can blackmail me? ME?" His voice was loud.

"She will do nothing of the sort," a voice said from behind my husband.

He turned, "Sal, I don't know what this woman has told you, but it is a lie."

"Oh yes," Sal smiled. "I was not so quick to set you aside, but she showed me the proof, and we found the Cayman account. Very tidy, very tidy indeed. I want you to know she asked for mercy for you, but you know I cannot offer that. When I explained that to her, she understood."

"Look Sal, we can make a deal," my husband pleaded. I thought about how he no longer looked like the monster he had been, the roles had changed, and he was now me.

"You would deal with what? Our money? Too late, account empty. You have nothing," Sal stated.

My husband launched at me, but Sal's men lept into the room and grabbed him in midair. "I will kill you," he seethed at me.

Sal smiled and handed me the envelope, "Is that Chicken Parmesan?" Sal asked while the two men held my husband on the floor. "It smells delicious."

I was embarrassed. "Yes, it is." I was confused a little. "Would you like some?"

"A small bite," Sal said. I cut a piece and handed him the fork. Sal took the fork and ate the piece. "Oh, that is heaven. Can you share the recipe with me before you leave town?"

"Of course." I held my head down again.

Sal reached out to my face, and I winced. He lifted my chin to look him in the eyes. "I know people like your husband. It is a shame they exist. You need never lower your eyes again. After tonight he will not exist. I have given you some money, but it appears he has an insurance policy as well.

After we discuss things with him, the insurance will pay out, and you will get the settlement. It will offer finality for you and your children. It will give my partners the justice they deserve. You will never face him alive again after tonight. Is there anything you would like to say to him?"

I thought about it. The years of pain. The intensity I felt. All of the agony I had been put through. I looked down at my husband's pleading eyes.

"Goodbye," I said and left the room.

Vacation

Jim had never won anything before. At this point, he was not expecting a vacation, let alone an all-expenses paid vacation to Hawaii. His divorce was close to final, and he knew the windfall he would make would be considerable. His wife did very well, and he expected to take half of her quite sizable fortune.

The flyer said the Hawaiian vacation would be the most impressive of his lifetime. Eight weeks of island tours and beach parties. Jim had called the number and was surprised that everything checked out. It wouldn't be unlike Victoria to plan some elaborate scheme to attempt to keep him from taking her money. Still, eight weeks away would not allow him to keep his job, and he was concerned.

"Don't worry," Jenna, the representative told him. "Everything will be taken care of, and you will get the check for $10,000 if you tour one of our fine villas."

That was all Jim had needed. He called in, quit his job, and got ready for a fantastic trip.

"This was sponsored by Amazing Glow Tanning, and you should pre-tan to ensure you won't get burnt in the Hawaiian sun. Amazing Glow has donated a free tan to ensure that your trip will be memorable and exciting. They guarantee you will be as dark as necessary." The representative said. "All you have to do is show up, give your name, and they'll take care of you. It is important you also tan on the day you leave and take a promotional shot with them. Then, they will give you your tickets."

"No problem," Jim laughed. "I'm gonna love this."

Jim arranged everything and made sure the house would be taken care of until it sold and that all of the utilities were paid up.

Amazing Glow Tanning turned out to be a highlight every day

for Jim. He enjoyed lying nude in the tanning bed and the tingle on his skin when he got out. The staff at Amazing Glow were attentive and ensured that his every need was met. Several of them talked to him about winning the trip and how lucky he was to be going to Hawaii. One of the women, Terri, told Jim that she was in line to go next and that it would be a trip for her to remember. She laughed with him as they talked about what it would feel like to spend eight weeks in paradise. He liked Terri and wondered if she would go with him. He set it aside since she was a little thick for his taste and looked him eye to eye.

After Jim's fourth visit, Amazing Glow offered him a complete facial. Their new line of custom masks would clean his pores like never before. Jim laughed and took the complete facial. Three women spent their time covering his face with an amazing mask, then peeling it away and showing him all of the impurities it had removed. The mask was unique as it came off in one piece.

"Wow, I look like a porcupine," Jim laughed.

Jim felt good. He almost wished he and Victoria could have shared this together. The thought slipped his mind rapidly as he smiled and wondered who he would meet in the tropical paradise he was about to visit. This would be heaven. This would be his life.

The last day came quickly. Jim was packed and ready to go. He had his passport and ID ready, even though he only needed his ID. It was in the rules, and who was he to care. Jim headed to the Amazing Glow Tanning location. He would get his last Tan, do his photo shoot, and head to paradise.

Terri and the team were there waiting for him.

"Your base tan is coming along perfectly." Terri said, "Let's get you in our deluxe room for your last tan. We'll get your photos done and send you on your way."

Jim smiled, his elation was real, and it felt good. He was about to be a rich man and then some.

He was led to a new room. The music played a little louder as Terri opened the bed for him. "As you can see, this room is meant for our special guests. Do you have a preference for music?"

"Something jazzy," Jim laughed. "With a little punch."

"Do you want it loud or soft?" Terri asked.

"I don't want to wake the neighbors," Jim began.

"This special room is soundproof, just for our special guests." Terri smiled.

"Then crank it; I am celebrating."

"Remove your clothes, and I will explain this bed," Terri stated.

"With you in here?" Jim asked.

"It's okay, I won't look." Terri winked.

Jim took off his clothes and hoped he was about to get lucky, but instead, the clothes were neatly folded and set to the side.

"Okay," Terri said. "This bed is a little tighter, but it will give you a tan that others will weep over. You will be an idol to everyone who sees you after this."

"I am ready," Jim said. "You will be going soon too, right?"

"Yes," Terri said. "My trip is right around the corner."

Jim got in the bed, and Terri pulled down the door with him. "It will feel tight, but it will only be for a few minutes."

Jim heard the bed lock, and the bulbs came on. The light blue glow was mesmerizing. Jim actually really liked tanning and was enjoying the warmth. His arm felt funny. He reached down. It was hot, too hot, and he was feeling a little strange. The bulbs became brighter and brighter still. Jim felt his face burn and sweat run across his brown.

"It's too hot!" Jim yelled. "This is too hot!"

Jim started pounding on the glass in the bed, but it was tight; he had no leverage. He strained against the roof of the bed and noticed blood covering some of the glass. The blood began to sizzle and pop. The bulbs began to get brighter. He felt his skin sizzle. He kicked and screamed with all his might.

"Let me out! Let me out!"

The sounds were echoing in his ears. He screamed a wail of pain, then was silent.

"It's perfect," Victoria said, looking at Jim's face in front of her. "I couldn't tell at all. How did you get it so realistic?"

"Easy," Jenna said. "During a full-face mask, we mapped his body down to each and every pore. This mask was created to be a perfect representation. It will be worn on the flight over and during the Villa Tour, and then it will be destroyed. Our representative, Terri, will stay the week and then take a cruise ship back. Jim's belongings will be left in his room, and he will be just another missing person."

"That may cause a problem," Victoria stated. "We have a court date."

"No," Jenna replied. "When he doesn't show up, the items will be shelved, and after he is reported missing from Hawaii, it will be a few months to a few years to settle, but it will not affect any of your assets."

"Genius," Victoria said. "As for the money?"

"You can't pay us in any lump amount. We have a sister company in cosmetics, and you will subscribe to their new line. I will send you a notice for the initial consult and meet you there. It will be easy to hide the payments with beauty supplies, and no large payout will be made to anyone. This will keep your banking strictly legitimate, and you will not be subject to any issues during an investigation. If there is one, there will be nothing to link to you. So far, we have had a zero percent investigation record."

"You have thought of everything. This is wonderful; just one more thing, what about the body?" Victoria asked.

Jenna nodded to a woman in the room that brought a small necklace to Victoria.

"You will get a necklace like this one, his ashes are being prepared now, and they will be heated to a high temperature and fused into a gemstone. The process will break down all DNA strands. His DNA has been destroyed in our special tanning bed. The LASER induction system literally forced more and more LASER light into the chamber until it fractured bonds. It was an accidentally discovered process that reduces human tissue to ash in a very short time. It was work that my husband had been doing, and I put to good use. You can keep the necklace or discard it; it will be up to you."

"Marvelous," Victoria replied. "I look forward to it."

Terri, dressed as Jim with the mask in place, said, "I need to catch a plane."

"So you do, so you do," Jenna replied, and the room rapidly emptied.

Jenna smiled at the gemstone left on her desk, "I'd like to say I miss you honey, but I don't. Thanks for helping me build a successful enterprise."

Edges

Alexandra Xavier Cross turned the page of the massive tome before her. The cuneiform script seemed to dance before her eyes as she stood in the rare book area of the library. The answers were somewhere, but they seemed to elude her like a scent in the wind. Her cane sat next to her, a reminder of a time only a few months ago when walking was a struggle. Her time now was spent looking for clues to the origin of the sword that saved her, and her friend Karen, and gave Alexandra the ability to walk again without pain.

Karen Klay walked into the area with her. Since their ordeal, Karen now sported short black pixie cut hair with blue tips. Alexandra remembered the night she found the sword, but to Karen it was a dimly painted dream. Her near-death experience with an overdose left gaps, but she still knew she had to change and had been trying. She still talked about her now ex-boyfriend but did not push or ask questions. She just knew he was gone, and she needed to clean up her life.

"I brought you a sandwich," Karen whispered.

"Again?" Alexandra replied as she continued studying the texts.

"You need to eat," Karen pleaded in a quiet voice.

"What I need to do is find information about my latest treasure," Alexandra replied. "If it wasn't for that sword, you wouldn't be alive right now."

"I still don't understand how that worked," Karen noted. "You said the sword saved me, but it seems like you saved me. Are you sure it just wasn't you?"

"Of course, I'm sure," Alexandra replied. "I know you don't believe me, but the sword has a special ability that I can't really explain. You've seen how I can walk now; did you ever expect that to even be a possibility?"

"No," Karen was thoughtful. "It's obvious there is something going on, but where does it get its power? Is it evil? How did you know how to use it? Maybe we should try to find Greg and get his take on what happened that night. You know he might be able to help."

"I don't think Greg will be any help," Alexandra said with certainty. "We haven't seen him since that night, and I am 100% sure that we will never see him again."

"It just isn't like him to run away like that," Karen said. "I mean, yeah, he's a jerk, but I thought he really liked me."

Alexandra was visibly annoyed. "If he really liked you, he wouldn't have put that crap in your veins. He could have killed you. If it wasn't for the sword, you would be dead right now."

"So you keep saying," Karen replied. "I have to get to class, but I love you, you bum."

"I love you too, you idiot," Alexandra replied. "Don't worry, I'm sure you'll find another guy to treat you just as bad."

"You're so sweet to me," Karen laughed. "Maybe I want to find a good guy this time. Maybe you need to find a good guy. You seem to dump anyone that is nice to you, and your type seems to be the ones that can't add 2 + 2 and get 4."

"This isn't about me, is it? Alexandra said as she turned the page on another large book. "When was the last time I went out with anyone?"

"I don't know," Karen said. "I think it was that guy, Daniel. Wasn't he the one that asked you why you had a cane?"

"No, that was another moron," Alexandra said. "Daniel was the one that had all the money in the world until we went out the first time and he asked me to pay for everything."

"Oh yeah," Karen laughed. "He was the one that talked about women paying being some sort of freedom of expression."

"Yeah, that's him," Alexandra replied. "You have to remember though, that was almost three years ago. I think I was a freshman then."

"God, that seems like such a long time ago," Karen said. "You need to eat. You need to take care of yourself. Why don't you meet me at the building after my class and I'll make you a good dinner."

"I guess," Alexandra laughed. "Maybe I should pick up sushi."

"Oh Yum," Karen smacked her lips, "That would be super awesome and tasty."

"Who says stuff like that?" Alexandra replied. "Super-awesome? That sounds like you've been doing those drugs again."

"I will have you know I've been clean since you saved me," Karen said. "I still don't know how I avoided going to the hospital. That was such an odd night. I remember dancing kind of, and I remember Greg and his friends, but I don't remember them leaving."

"That's because I was going to kick their asses if they didn't leave," Alexandra said. "You need to stay away from people that want to hurt you. I told Greg if he came back, I would use the sword on him in his sleep."

"He probably thought you were gonna give him a Lorena Bobbitt," Karen laughed.

Karen began walking out of the room, and Alexandra stopped laughing. She hated lying to her friend about everything that happened. How could she tell Karen that the sword got its power from the lives of those it killed? How could she explain that she killed Greg so that Karen could live? It still baffled her, and she had found no trace in any of the books all the way back to the time of Jesus Christ. She closed the book in front of her and shook her head. The cuneiform that was in this book was far older than the Roman Empire. The box that she opened by solving the puzzle had Roman numerals on it, and there had to be something in Greek or Roman mythology to point to the origin of the blade.

She took the bound book back to a shelf where she found it. She really had no place to continue. She had gone through hundreds of books on ancient weapons and dozens specifically on swords in the last several months. There was nothing even close to the design of the sword. There was no mention anywhere of a sword with magical powers or special properties or even one that held an edge longer than another besides Excalibur. She wrote about Excalibur for a while and wondered if her sword was similar to the sword of legend, but there were no properties even similar in the tales of Arthur and the Knights of the round table.

Alexandra heard the click of heels behind her and turned to greet the middle-aged librarian who frequented the rare book area.

"You look frustrated," Marjorie said. "You've gone through all of these books, and you can't seem to find what you're looking for?"

"Well, I haven't gone through them all, obviously," Alexandra replied. "But I've gone through the ones on specific topics that I was interested in. I'm just not sure where to go from here. I'm looking for ancient mythology, but I can't even tell you the era I am interested in."

"Can you give me some idea of what type of myth you are looking for?" Marjorie asked.

"I'm looking at ancient weapons for a paper on how mythology and reality intersect," Alexandra lied. "I was hoping to find something about ancient weapons that may have had special abilities."

"What type of special abilities are you looking for?" Marjorie asked. "If we look at the time of Perseus, he was given a special sword that was impervious. That sword was named Harpe and was so sharp and strong it took the head of a Gorgon. The sword named Durendal was supposedly capable of slicing through solid rock. There are several swords in Muslim lore that were as powerful. There are also the swords of Shiva and Kali that were supposed to have special properties as well, but there is very little available on that. It seems that swords of true power are often shrouded in mystery, and those that wield them are not so anxious to have them in the history books.”

“I'm impressed that you know so much about it,” Alexandra was fascinated, “Don't you think there would be some record somewhere of a sword that had a more unique ability?”

“I'm sure there's some book of fiction that has a sword that can let you fly or do something else that is truly amazing, but I would like to believe that anything potentially dangerous or that had something unique attached to it would be hidden from public view. Think about artifacts like the spear of destiny. The Bible has some information on it, but when you consider all of the myths surrounding the spear of destiny, no one really knows if it has extra abilities now.”

“Do you believe in things like that?” Alexandra asked.

“Well, of course I do,” Marjorie replied. “Think about it. There are so many things that we see daily that are utter miracles and can't be explained by science. After all, science tries to explain away things that just can't easily be explained. We have literature about amazing creatures like Dragons from all over the world, but science says they never existed. Science can't really grasp the world unless the world is black and white.”

Alexandra nodded. “I agree with you, but I still would like something special for my paper. Any ideas?”

“Oh, heavens no,” Marjorie replied. “My imagination just isn't that fantastic. I surround myself with all of these books, and I could no more write them than you could.”

"Have you ever heard of anything that I could use?" Alexandra pressed. "Like, is there any legend of a sword that pulls down lightning, or parts the waters, or heals people?"

"My, you do have a good imagination," Marjorie laughed. "You should get on the Internet and just look up famous swords. I'm sure you could use Excalibur or a few that I have mentioned and do just fine with your paper."

"Okay," Alexandra said. "I'll do just that. I really appreciate your help, Marjorie; it would be awesome if you see something, if you could let me know."

"Have you ever seen a sword up close?" Marjorie asked.

"Yes, of course," Alexandra replied. "I collect a variety of strange items, and I have an old katana that I studied closely."

"It is amazing how a sword can become an extension of your arm or even part of a dance. A good sword will be so balanced that you can feel it slide through the air." Marjorie seemed almost hypnotized. "Imagine a sword built just for you that would allow you to transcend the idea of life and death. It's kind of a given assumption that's swords take life, but perhaps that energy can be harnessed."

Alexandra was staring at Marjorie, "That sounds very intriguing. You have a very colorful imagination."

Marjorie looked down at the floor. "Yes, I suppose I do. I hope you find something that inspires you."

Marjorie spun on her heels and walked rapidly out of the area. Alexandra was suddenly filled with a little dread and wondered how Marjorie had come so close to describing what she had found. Should Alexandra open up to Marjorie and see if she knows about her sword?

Alexandra was the one that stared at the floor now. Questions were going through her mind. She wondered how that simple librarian made the leap to a sword of life and death. Alexandra also wondered if there was something else that put Marjorie into her trance for those few minutes.

Alexandra decided to leave. She could take her time walking back to her building and clean up a little. The discussion with Marjorie made her uneasy, but she couldn't decide why. She took her backpack and cane and walked down the stairs to the front door. As she reached the front door, she looked back into the library and the balcony that housed the rare books. She saw that Marjorie was watching her as she left. The hair on the back of Alexandra's neck stood up. She felt uncomfortable under Marjorie's gaze. Still, Alexandra turned and walked out of the building.

It was harder now for Alexandra to walk with her cane. Since her leg was now more than fully healed, she was stronger than most men twice her size. Feigning the limp that she had always displayed was becoming more and more difficult. Her body now seemed to have a natural rhythm, and she wanted to just throw the cane down and walk. How could she explain to the school and to everyone that knew her, that her magical sword had healed her body? How many doctors would beg for the secret to reverse a genetic flaw and make someone whole again?

Twilight was coming. The sky was full of pinks, purples, and wild shades of blue. To the west, there were crimson streaks of light reflecting from the puffy clouds. The sunset was awe-inspiring. Alexandra now enjoyed the sunset where previously it just meant another night of pain.

Alexandra heard the click of heels behind her. She turned but no one was there, and the click stopped. Alexandra kept walking and once again heard the click of heels. She glanced behind again and saw nothing. She kept her pace and continued the charade of her leg not working well. She turned left at the next block and ran directly into Marjorie.

"Hello, Alexandra," Marjorie said.

"Um, hello," Alexandra replied. "How did you get in front of me?"

"I walked another way, and I'm a fast walker," Marjorie said. "I was thinking about your question about swords and wondered if there was something else there?"

"No," Alexandra noted. "It's just an assignment. I just want it to be perfect."

"It seems more like an obsession," Marjorie replied. "I've been watching you for quite some time, and you continue to look for the same things. This is far beyond an assignment."

"No," Alexandra emphasized. "It's just an assignment. It's not a big deal."

Alexandra began to walk around Marjorie but then kicked the cane out from under her. Alexandra stood fast.

"Why did you do that?" Alexandra asked.

"I've noticed that your gait comes and goes now. If I remember correctly, you have a degenerative disease, and your legs should be getting much worse. I read a lot, and I know there is no cure for your disease. You'll have to forgive me, but I did a little research on you and looked up the exact disease that you have. Now you're standing here with no cane, and you barely flinched. There's a reason you're asking about swords, isn't there? There's a reason for all of this?"

"You have Balance, don't you?" Marjorie asked.

"What are you talking about?" Alexandra replied as she backed away.

"Where is the Sword of Balance?" Marjorie pushed and crowded Alexandra towards the nearby building. "If it is not the Sword of Balance, which one is it?"

"I have no idea what you're talking about," Alexandra said.

"Let's find out," Marjorie said. She reached to her right, opening her palm and extending it as she closed her eyes for a brief moment. A sword appeared in her hand, pointing towards the sky. The blade was long, at least forty-eight inches, and the hilt golden and ornate. It was not like the sword Alexandra found but instead was more traditional.

"Tell me where the Sword of Balance is, and I will let you live," Marjorie said.

"What are you talking about?" Alexandra asked.

"I know you have the sword," Marjorie replied. "There's no other explanation for how you were healed. It all makes sense. Your obsession with swords and the idea that there are swords, or at least a sword, with a special ability."

"Maybe I just want to learn more about swords," Alexandra continued to back away.

"Oh, I don't think so," Marjorie replied. "You have one, don't you? Or at least you know where it is."

"Marjorie, I think you're nuts," Alexandra replied. "You have been around too many books and lost a few screws along the way."

The swing was silent, and the golden hilted sword swung at her with impossible grace. Still, it was almost slow motion to Alexandra, and she rolled out of the way and jumped backward ten feet.

"Do you see how easy that was? Do you see now there is no way you could do what you just did? I would have cleaved a normal person in half. Answer my question where is the sword?" Marjorie asked.

"I'm curious where you were hiding yours," Alexandra was stalling, hoping someone would walk up on them.

"You really don't know anything about it, do you?" Marjorie stared into Alexandra's eyes "You think you found the sword, or that you picked it up, or chose it. The sword found you. The sword is tied to its owner, and it is a relationship that transcends mortal comprehension. When I call to my sword, it is there. My sword is beyond time and space and allows me to live."

"You're sounding awfully crazy again," Alexandra stalled.

"I'm not crazy," Marjorie screamed with insane energy. "I've had this sword for hundreds of years, and I have never come across any of the others that are out there. I thought the old texts were wrong until you came into the library, and I saw your passion for finding proof."

"So, there is a sword like this? I'll be able to write my paper.?" Alexandra chided. "I'm curious where the old texts are, of course."

"There is no proof they even exist. The advantage of being in the education system and of course a librarian; it gives me the ability to slowly eliminate those things that could incriminate me. There were only a few dozen books that mentioned the seven. Those few dozen are now either destroyed or safe with me." Marjorie swung again with more purpose. As the blade came down, Alexandra dove out of the way again, and Marjorie's sword cut the brick wall. Alexandra looked at the wall. It was as though molten fire had gone through it and melted the brick.

"That's a neat trick," Alexandra said.

"Tell me where the sword is, so I don't have to kill you," Marjorie huffed.

"Lady, I don't know what you're talking about," Alexandra challenged.

"Liar!" Marjorie barked and moved rapidly, shoving Alexandra against the wall. "Perhaps your roommate will be more cooperative." Marjorie punched Alexandra in the stomach.

Alexandra dropped to her knees and gasped. She was surprised. Ever since the night she used the sword, her sword, nothing had been able to hurt her.

"I can go ahead and kill you and just take my time with your roommate. You have just confirmed again that you have the sword or one of them because a normal person would have been dead from that punch. I have snapped a man in half with my punch."

Alexandra stood up and let her hair fall where it may. "It was a good punch." She swung her fist directly into Marjorie's face with lightning speed. Marjorie fell back overtop of herself and hit the ground hard. "How's mine?"

Marjorie stood up and eyed Alexandra. A drop of blood was evident in the crease of her mouth. Marjorie stuck out her tongue and licked the blood away, then wiped her face. Her hair was mussed. The look in her eyes was no longer the look of control but instead the fire of anger and unrestrained passion. "Not bad. It has been hundreds of years since I was hit that hard."

Marjorie swung her sword again in a wide arc, coming towards Alexandra. Alexandra dove backward, avoiding the blade. She knew her blade could be fatal with even a minor cut; she did not want to take the chance that this sword was as deadly. As those thoughts went through her mind, she realized that even a blade with no special ability would be deadly with the right owner. It seemed Marjorie had been with this blade for a long time. Alexandra continued to avoid her by keeping a distance. She could not go on the offensive without being closer, and the sword seemed to have a life of its own as it tried to get to her.

Alexandra's cane lay on the ground, to her left. The steel shaft might give her the ability to be more aggressive. In a series of parries, Alexandra worked her way over to the cane and picked it up. Marjorie smiled as she swung again, and Alexandra used the cane to block the sword, only to watch it split in half with no effort. The attack and attempted defense put Alexandra off balance, and she fell to the ground. Marjorie advanced and swung her sword directly at Alexandra's head.

There was a splitting sound reminiscent of two trains colliding at full speed and an explosion of sparks. Alexandra's sword was now in her hand.

"Well, that's new," Alexandra said. "It appears that you no longer have the advantage."

Marjorie saw the red hilt, the sleek blade, and the sharpened quillons sparkling in the still twilight sky. "I thought you would have the Sword of Balance," Marjorie said. "It appears you have the Sword of Fury."

"Fury," Alexandra said. "I like the sound of that."

Alexandra swung her sword in a high arc, coming down on Marjorie but Marjorie blocked it with earth-shattering sound. A slide and a turn, and Alexandra came back with a second blow, and this time Marjorie parried sideways and again blocked. Without pause, Alexandra swung again with what could only be described as fury. The two swords locked as the quillons approached each other. Marjorie's eyes opened wide as she saw the bladed quillons of the Sword of Fury moving closer to her. She moved to lock those edges away from her. Alexandra pivoted, flinging Marjorie's sword to the ground.

"Not possible," Marjorie said. "You are just a child."

"Well, I am a pissed off child with lots of issues," Alexandra replied.

There were sounds of people in the distance. The clash of the two swords was almost cinematic and sure to draw a crowd as they narrowed in on the disturbance.

Marjorie closed her eyes for a second, and her sword was in her hand again. She looked around and backed away, then ran.

"What's the matter Marjorie?" Alexandra asked. "Not interested in playing with a fair fight?"

It was too late. Marjorie turned the corner and was gone. Alexandra looked down at the sword in her hand and was astonished at how good it felt. "Fury huh?" she asked no one in particular, except perhaps the sword. "How am I going to get you back home without being seen?"

There was a blink of light, and the sword was gone.

Alexandra picked up her cane, now neatly split in two, grabbed her backpack, and walked home. She was careful to limp along the way. Almost immediately, people ran into the alleyway and asked if she had seen anything. She shook her head and made her way to her place.

The building was dark in the twilight, but the LED lights came on as she approached, lighting the whole area. The light wasn't much, but it made her feel safe. Alexandra made her way to the freight elevator. She did not feel the adrenaline as she thought she would. Instead, she felt very peaceful and wondered how she could find any of the books that obviously had been stolen away from history. As she reached her floor and walked out of the elevator. Karen was there.

"Class let out early, and I'm already making dinner. It's good that you came home. Did you find anything about your mystery sword?" Karen asked.

"Actually, I found out quite a lot and learned some cool new things. However, in the process, I almost got killed, and somewhere along the way I almost got you killed, but I guess that comes with the territory," Alexandra said with a flippant smile.

"You know you should write books with all the wild ideas you come up with," Karen said. "Our life just has never been that exciting."

"Maybe that's all about to change," Alexandra replied. "I'll be back in a few minutes."

Alexandra went to her room and walked over to the box she had mounted on the wall with the puzzle on the front and aligned them into VIXI. The box clicked, and Alexandra opened it. The sword was there as though it had never left. She took it out and felt the warmth in her hand. It was a magnificent sword. Marjorie said the sword had chosen her. Inside, Alexandra knew that they had chosen each other.

In the other room, Karen yelled that dinner was ready. Alexandra put the sword back and closed the combination. There was now a clue to the sword's origin, and she knew that Marjorie would not be at the library again. It would be up to Alexandra to find this woman and figure out what they both had, where the swords came from, and the purpose of her life. As she put the case back on the wall, she smiled. "From Death, Life." She thought it had been an inscription describing the sword's purpose but instead realized that the sword was all the fury in between.

Loyal

New York City was not as I expected. I had only been there a few weeks when I realized all the things I missed from home. My Mom and Dad, sister, brother, and of course, my dog, Shadow. I wish I could have brought Shadow with me, but it was not to be. The apartment I rented was overpriced and did not allow pets. There were days that I expected it to say 'no tenants' as well. The rattling pipes, thin walls, and horrible heating made me long for home and my old apartment, only a short run from the house.

I was happy when I found a position back in my hometown and got ready to move back. My mom was particularly happy about it. Having a supportive family is more than a little awesome. She was counting down the moments to my being home. I was looking forward to home-cooked meals, family fun, and having Shadow curl up with me on the couch, watching TV. I think of all the things I missed, I missed Shadow the most simply because she had grown up with me.

We got Shadow when I was ten, and she named herself in a matter of hours. Everywhere I went, she was right there with me. When I watched TV she watched with me. When I read a book, she was there. I tripped over her a lot, but it wasn't a big deal. It broke my heart to leave her when I got the UI position in New York. I requested that the position be remote, but they were adamant. The job had to be in person.

Now I would be back in Indiana with family, friends, and Shadow. My life would be on the right track again.

The truck came and loaded me up. I called Mom to let her know I was coming home. I let her know I would be driving in tonight and would come by the house in the morning. The truck would unload, and I had it all planned so I would have the whole day tomorrow with family. It was a good deal. My new position gave me a big enough bonus to get the truck and drive home with it. Labor would meet me there, and they would take the truck back, leaving me at the apartment.

I drove straight through, and it was long eleven-hour drive. I avoided stopping as I had labor set for 6:00 PM to unload my meager belongings. I called Mom along the way and let her know how I was doing and told her not to bother with anything. I told her that I would be fine, and I'd see her in the morning. She pushed, as did the rest of my family, to come over and help, but I made my own mess and wanted to clean it up. I wanted the place to be before they came over.

Amazingly, I rolled into the apartment complex at 5:55 PM. There were two men waiting by an old red pickup truck wearing a branded T-shirt that sported their company logo. Unloading was quick, and by 7:30 PM I was handing them cash and going into my new apartment. It didn't take me long to set up the couch and the television and make sure that I could relax. I took a few more minutes and put sheets on the bed that the two men had already set up. I was putting things away and stacking up cardboard boxes when I heard a scratch at the door. I walked to the door and opened it to see Shadow.

Shadow was a small German shepherd of about sixty pounds. She looked at me with her chocolate brown eyes and walked into the apartment as though she belonged there. I looked out and saw no one but figured Mom and Dad had dropped her off as a surprise. It was a good surprise.

Tail wagging and actually whole butt wagging we had our reunion. I hugged her, and held her, and didn't want to let go. My face was cleaned thoroughly, and I thought I was going to drown in all the puppy kisses. I was in heaven.

If you haven't had a good dog, you have missed out. Shadow was the best. We unpacked a few more boxes together until I found the popcorn. Then I plugged in the microwave and made a package of Orville Redenbacher's buttered popcorn. Our favorite. I grabbed a big bowl and walked to the couch where Shadow plopped down next to me, looking up with eager eyes.

I clicked on the TV and found a dumb movie on my complimentary cable box. Shadow and I shared popcorn one bite at a time. She was still awesome. I tossed the popcorn in the air, and she caught each and every bite. It wasn't long until we ran out. We sat there watching the movie together; me with my foot propped up on a box and Shadow with her head on my lap.

It had been a long day, and this was the best welcome home present I could ever have. I fell asleep with my hand on Shadow's head, feeling her warmth on my leg. I dreamed good dreams of growing up and playing catch with Shadow in the park.

When I awoke in the morning, I was alone. I realized the door was cracked open and knew that home was only a few blocks away. I put away our popcorn bowl and took a quick shower. I had to stop and dig out a towel while running around the house naked. A few minutes later, I was dressed and ready to head home. I walked outside to the refreshing morning Indiana air. I stretched a little and then began first a light walk, and then a steady jog to my childhood home. I glanced at the businesses in the quaint downtown area along the way. All the memories of my childhood came back to me. I should have never left but I was starting out on a fantastic journey here at home.

I got to the house and walked in. I yelled for Mom and Dad. They walked out of the kitchen and hugged me. It was a wonderful reunion. I was home. I asked where Shadow had gotten off to. Mom looked down at the floor. It was my dad that broke the silence.

"Son, Shadow passed away yesterday afternoon. We took her to the vet and didn't want to tell you on the phone. I'm sorry."

I was stunned. "Dad, Mom. Shadow was with me last night. We watched a movie together and ate popcorn. She fell asleep on my lap."

My mom and dad looked at each other and then looked back at me. "Son, that's not possible."

I sat there dumbfounded for a moment. Then I smiled. Of course, I was sad, but I also was happy. Shadow held on for a few more hours and was there for me to make my homecoming perfect. I would miss her every day because she was loyal to the end and somewhere beyond. I would hold her in my heart because she was there, no matter what.

About the Author

Andrew Allen Smith was born in Anderson, Indiana. Until the age of fifteen, he moved at least once per year and finally settled in Lexington, Kentucky. Andrew spent a significant amount of his teenage years reading and writing short stories and poetry. He published his first book, "A Slice of Passion," in 2005. It was a book of poetry compiled from dozens of years of work.

In 2015, Andrew published "The Theft and Other Short Stories" as a collection of some of his favorites after he was challenged to self-publish a book. Challenged and excited about his success, he published his first novel, "Vengeful Son," in 2016 and began building a franchise with that book. "The Masterson Files" (the series containing "Vengeful Son") now includes five books and has fifteen in outline form. The story follows an ex-assassin that is reluctantly engaged to help others while trying to retire.

In 2020, after a tragic event, Andrew co-wrote "What NOT to Say to People Who Are Grieving." This book was a showcase of emotions and an approach to helping others be more mindful of their words during grief.

As a quality engineer and system architect, Andrew's work also gave him credit for a series of instructional manuals for site relationship management systems, a variety of quality documents, and development lifecycles. In Andrew's spare time, he has a passion for a considerable number of hobbies and his family, which he considers paramount. For more information about Andrew, please visit andrewallensmith.com.

Books by Andrew Allen Smith

Fiction
A Slice of Passion
A Slice of Fear
Another Slice of Fear
The Theft and Other Short Stories

The Masterson Files Series
Vengeful Son
Sinful Father
Deadly Daughter
Fateful Friend
Silent Sister

The Eternal Forever Series
Adam

Non-Fiction
What NOT to say to People Who are Grieving

Books Containing Andrew Allen Smith's prose
Monster Hunter – Intern
Simple Things
The Portrait of Herbert Losh and Other Stories

Coming Soon
Burial Ground
Stealth Drive
The Masterson Files Book 6 - Curious Cousin
The Eternal Forever Book 2 – Morgan
Another Slice of Passion